HAND TO HAND ON ALIEN SOIL!

Peel's team was to assault the citadel. Waiting was going to do no good. If the enemy was inside, then waiting just gave him time to prepare a better defense. And if he wasn't, then waiting just gave rise to unnecessary anxiety. Peel yelled, "Let's take them!"

Two soldiers ran forward, slapped plastic explosive on one of the doors and darted away. An instant later there was a quiet hissing, a pop, and the door fell in. The soldiers threw grenades in.

And the grenades came sailing right back out, a mushrooming of snow and dark brown dirt. There was a scream from inside. The enemy rushed from the building, firing lasers at the humans. Their blue and yellow beams slashed through the night, smashing into the surprised soldiers. Just one soldier stood his ground. A half dozen of the enemy ran at him. . . .

Ace Books by Kevin Randle

Jefferson's War Series

THE GALACTIC SILVER STAR
THE PRICE OF COMMAND
THE LOST COLONY
THE JANUARY PLATOON
DEATH OF A REGIMENT
CHAIN OF COMMAND

JEFFERSON'S WAR
CHAIN OF COMMAND

KEVIN RANDLE

ACE BOOKS, NEW YORK

This book is an Ace original edition,
and has never been previously published.

CHAIN OF COMMAND

An Ace Book / published by arrangement with
the author

PRINTING HISTORY
Ace edition / March 1992

All rights reserved.
Copyright © 1992 by Kevin Randle.
Cover art by Paul Youll.
This book may not be reproduced in whole or in part,
by mimeograph or any other means, without permission.
For information address: The Berkley Publishing Group,
200 Madison Avenue, New York, New York 10016.

ISBN: 0-441-38442-0

Ace Books are published by The Berkley Publishing Group,
200 Madison Avenue, New York, New York 10016.
The name "ACE" and the "A" logo
are trademarks belonging to Charter Communications, Inc.

PRINTED IN THE UNITED STATES OF AMERICA

10 9 8 7 6 5 4 3 2 1

1

BRIGADIER GENERAL DAVID Steven Jefferson sat at the head of the long conference table and surveyed the remains of his staff. Victoria Torrence, once the executive officer of the Tenth Interplanetary Infantry, sat on his immediate right. Opposite her was Major Michael Carter, the bandage around his right hand barely visible under his tunic sleeve.

The only other military man in the room was Joseph Tyson. He was not a combat officer, but an anthropologist who had been assigned to the regiment. Next to him was the journalist, Jason Garvey, who had survived the disastrous battle by remaining on the ships of the fleet, though the fleet hadn't done very well either.

Jefferson shook his head finally and then stared down at the highly polished hardwood of the conference table. For an instant, he let his mind roam, deciding that it was a waste of time, effort and energy to lift a mahogany table into orbit and then transport it through space so that the general would have a nice table for his meetings. There were so many better ways to spend the money.

Then, looking up at the assembled staff, he said, "We're all that remains, with the exception of a handful of enlisted soldiers, from the Tenth Interplanetary Infantry. Nineteen of us made it."

He studied the others, but couldn't read their faces. He felt an overwhelming grief suddenly, believing that he'd failed the regiment in some fashion. The men and women who had made up the body of the regiment had died defending a worthless planet a dozen light years from Earth, hoping to prevent a spacefaring enemy they'd rarely seen from invading the cradle of the human race.

Jefferson turned away and looked at the holo near the bulkhead that represented space outside the ship. They were orbiting the planet they had protected. Now the majority of the Army and Navy had joined them in a massive fleet that was about to launch itself into the great battle that could end the enemy threat once and for all.

But all Jefferson could see was the smoking remains of the base, the bodies of his regiment stacked around it. He could hear the cries of the wounded and dying. At night, in his cabin, with the radio turned up, the computer humming and with the intercom relaying every message from the bridge, he could still hear the voices of his dying regiment.

Late at night, in the dark, he could see the battle as the enemy overran his positions and killed the regiment. He saw it all, projected on the walls and ceiling as if he were still living it.

And although they had won the battle, the cost had been too high. Jefferson wondered what quirk of fate had allowed him to survive while so many others had died. It wasn't as if he'd been safely hidden in the bowels of the communications bunker or had been on a ship with the fleet. He'd been down there in the thick of it, fighting the enemy in the hand-to-hand battle that had decided the victory.

"General," said Torrence gently.

Jefferson looked at her and nodded. "Yes." He was quiet for a moment longer and then said, "Today we meet with the replacements."

He wanted to say more but couldn't think of the words. Replacements made it sound as if the regiment had survived the battle. Replacements made it sound as if a hundred new troops were being added to fill in gaps in the TO & E, when the fact was that nearly everyone in the regiment was new. The regiment that Jefferson had led into the battle had ceased to exist during the fighting. The Tenth Interplanetary Infantry, now under the command of Colonel Victoria Torrence, was not the same unit that it had been under Jefferson's command. Everything about it was different.

Jefferson, now a brigade commander with three regiments under his control, had been convinced that he would be court-martialed after the battle. Instead, he was honored and promoted. And as had happened when he won the Galatic Silver Star, he believed that his success had been purchased with the blood of others.

"General," said Torrence again.

"There isn't much to say," said Jefferson. He glanced at Carter. "You'll be assigned to my staff, if you desire to remain here."

"Certainly, General."

Looking at Garvey, he said, "Mister Garvey, you are free to take your video camera elsewhere. There isn't much left here to report."

Garvey grinned and in a voice that was too loud for the small cabin, said, "Not likely. You seem to draw the action. I'll stay with you."

"As you wish," said Jefferson. There was a quiet bong and he glanced down at the computer terminal. A message scrolled across it.

"It seems," he announced, "that the new troops are arriving. We should go down to the shuttle bay to meet them unless one of you has a question."

Torrence said, "No, General."

"Then you're dismissed."

Garvey and Carter stood but Torrence didn't move. As soon as they were out of the conference room, she asked, "Are you okay, David?"

Jefferson took a deep breath and looked at the woman who had been his executive officer during the months he'd commanded the Tenth Interplanetary Infantry. She was a handsome woman, five foot seven, with long brown hair and bright blue eyes. There was a new scar on her right cheek and her right shoulder slumped unnaturally, but that was a result of her wounds. She had trained to become an officer and had risen rapidly, partly due to Jefferson's ability to find the worst assignments and then to execute them flawlessly. Or, at the very least, succeed at them when it wasn't likely that anyone could succeed.

"Am I okay?" asked Jefferson, quietly. "I am responsible for the deaths of more than a thousand of my fellows in that battle. . . ."

"And responsible for the destruction of the enemy invasion force," said Torrence. "You sacrificed the regiment so that the Earth would be safe. A fair trade."

"You'll excuse me if I don't see it in quite those terms," Jefferson said.

"General . . . David. You can't keep blaming yourself."

"I don't need you to tell me that," said Jefferson.

Torrence shrugged. "Fine." She stood up. "If you'd screwed up as badly as you want to believe, they'd have posted you off to some remote area where you could have finished your career quietly. They wouldn't have promoted you and given you command of a brigade, no matter how many medals you have."

"I don't need a lecture from you."

"You need one from someone."

"Not from you," said Jefferson. "You don't know what command is. You have no idea what it is. But now you're going to learn about it."

"I've been close to command for the last few years," she said. "I know."

Jefferson turned to face the holo. A ship broke from the fleet, dropped into the planet's atmosphere and vanished. Jefferson didn't know if it was a real-time event or something that had been recorded and then broadcast.

Torrence moved closer to him and looked down. "Commanders have lost men and women from the dawn of time. It happens in war. It's the name of the game."

"Don't patronize me," said Jefferson.

"You're wasting time and effort," she said, her voice rising.

"You're becoming ridiculous. You don't see the division commander sitting around moping."

"He didn't issue the orders that killed two regiments," said Jefferson.

"Oh, hell," snapped Torrence. "There's no talking to you." She stomped to the hatch, stopped, and then ducked, disappearing into the corridor.

Jefferson watched her go and then turned back to the holo. He wondered if he was overplaying his role. Men and women died in combat. That was the way it was. It was the way that it had always been. There was nothing he could do about it. And it wasn't as if he'd ordered them into the fight and then remained behind where he would be safe.

He sat there thinking about it. Men and women had died, but not because he'd made a mistake. He'd done what had to be done to slow the enemy's progress toward Earth. He'd turned them around, inflicting so many casualties that the enemy had retired from the field and retreated from the system. His mission had been accomplished, and that was all that history ever remembered.

Now that he was off the planet and could reflect on the battle from the distance of a couple of weeks, he wondered if his emotional response wasn't the response that he believed others expected. Was the depression, the gloom he felt, the result of his belief that others expected it? A commander disgraced. That was the role he was playing.

But almost no one else believed it. Torrence was right. He had been promoted and given not one regiment, but three. If he had failed as badly as he thought he had, he would have been sent back to Earth to command a supply facility where no one could get hurt.

"All right," he said suddenly. "All right." He stood, glanced at the regimental flag, the new streamer denoting the last battle already hung from it.

Suddenly he felt proud. His regiment had performed well, and even in the last moments, when it was obvious that all was lost, the men and women continued to fight, taking as many of the enemy with them as they could. They had been well trained and very brave. It was all that could be asked of a regiment.

Jefferson left the conference room, the gloom that had hovered over him suddenly gone. He stepped out into a corridor lined with armed men and women, a reminder that a state of war still existed.

He hurried down it, found the mid-lift and descended toward the shuttle bay where the recruits would be forming. Outside the hatch to the shuttle bay, he found Torrence, along with the two new commanders of the other two new regiments, the eighth and the ninth. Both officers looked as if they were about thirty, had seen some combat, and had been cut from the same mold. Both were ramrod straight, had dark hair and dark eyes. The only real differences between them was that one was black and one was white, and one was male and the other was female. It was a strange phenomenon.

Jefferson nodded at them but didn't say a word. Instead he pulled Torrence to the side and whispered to her, "It's a good thing that we've served together before. Otherwise I'd have you up on charges for insubordination."

For an instant she looked grim and then quietly said, "Don't hand me a line of bullshit."

Jefferson nodded as the hatch irised open. Through it, he could see the shuttles, looking like giant black eggs squatting on four stumpy legs sitting on the deck. The replacements were still exiting the craft, forming into loose ranks as the officers and the NCOs tried to get them into a parade-ground formation.

Canned music blared from the control room. A few soldiers marched in time to it. The standard and flag bearers stood in front of the arriving troops looking as if they had been cast in bronze.

Jefferson stood for a moment and let the sights and sounds wash over him. He could see another such event that had taken place months before with soldiers who were now dead. But somehow that event no longer seemed important. The present belonged to the living and not those who had died.

Ducking, Jefferson stepped into the shuttle bay. To the right was the reviewing stand. Already there were a couple of colonels on its awaiting the arrival of the rest of the division staff.

Leaning close to Torrence, Jefferson said, "You know that the troops just want to get to their quarters and stretch out, relax and then sleep. They don't want welcoming speeches."

"Then don't make one," said Torrence.

Jefferson, with his three regimental commanders, walked across the deck and climbed the reviewing stand. One of the colonels, an old fat man who had spent his career in personnel management, asked, "Where's your medal, General?"

Jefferson shrugged and said, "Didn't think that it was appropriate here."

"The commander is going to want to see it," said the colonel.

Jefferson was about to say "sorry" and then remembered that he outranked the colonel now. There was no reason to worry about what he thought. Jefferson decided to ignore the comment.

Moments later the division commander entered the shuttle bay. He walked rapidly across the deck, climbed up on the reviewing stand, but said nothing to the officers waiting there. He raised a hand and the music ended. Now the shuttle bay echoed with the commands as the officers tried to force the recruits into proper formations.

In seconds it was quiet in the shuttle bay. The troops stood at attention, facing the reviewing stand. The division commander stood in front of them, surveying them slowly. Jefferson stood to his right, trying to see the faces of the newcomers. The only thing he noticed was that all of them seemed so damned young.

"Ladies and gentlemen," boomed the general, "officers and NCOs. Everyone. Welcome." He paused, let the echoes of his words die away and then resumed. "We are about to embark on a great adventure. One that will take us to the edges of the explored galaxy. There we will meet and engage an enemy whose existence threatens all human life."

Jefferson, standing there listening, was surprised that the commander would tell the incoming troops so much about the upcoming mission. He had been schooled by the intelligence officers who believed that you never said more than you had to. Too many ears provided too many opportunities for leaks.

But then, thinking about it, Jefferson wondered who they would tell. It wasn't as if anyone human was in contact with those who had attacked.

With half his mind, he listened as the general ran through his speech, trying to convince the newcomers that the coming fight was a great adventure. Jefferson had seen enough action to recognize the lie for what it was.

The general ran down, glanced back at the others on the stand, but gave them no chance to speak. Instead, he ordered, "Commanders, take charge of your units, and see that they are properly billeted. Officer's call for all those above the rank of major will be held at seventeen hundred hours."

Without another word, the commanding general swept off the reviewing stand and disappeared through the hatch. Torrence moved close to Jefferson and asked, "What in the hell was that all about?"

"Looks like we're going to get the word about five this afternoon."

"I don't think I care for that," said Torrence.

"Neither do I."

2

CAPTAIN JONATHAN RAMEY watched as one platoon from his company filtered into the squad bay. It looked as if the room was filled with coffins, but Ramey knew the coffins were stacked personal containment pods. The soldiers fanned out, in squad order, threw their gear into a pod and then turned, standing at attention.

Ramey had spent four years in a military school on Earth and then entered the army with a commission. He'd never spent a day on active duty as an enlisted trooper and therefore never had to spend a night in one of the pods. He'd once thought about it, just to see what it was like, but then had chickened out. He just couldn't crawl into such a confined space.

Ramey was a young man, only twenty-six. He was tall, slender and athletic. His blond hair was cut short and his blue eyes were piercing. There were no observable scars on his face or hands. And although he'd been serving in the army for three years, he had never been off Earth until he'd been tapped for his current assignment.

"Troops are all squared away, Captain."

Ramey turned and looked at his executive officer, Susan Crowley. That was another thing that bothered him. She was such a good-looking woman that he sometimes found it difficult to concentrate on the tasks at hand. Even with her hair cut short as it now was, and even wearing the standard coverall, it was obvious that she was beautiful. Ramey forced the thought from his mind.

"That include all platoons?"

"Yes, sir. All platoons."

Ramey glanced at his wristwatch. The ruby-colored numbers glowed at him. "Make sure that they get something to eat, and then let them have the rest of the day off. We'll begin tomorrow with breakfast at zero seven hundred."

"There are a couple of minor drills I'd like to pull tonight. They won't be expecting them. Give us a chance to see them react when completely surprised."

Ramey grinned broadly but shook his head. "I remember that happening in college all too often. Never taught us much but sure pissed us off. There's no need for it tonight. Let's give them a pass."

"Sir, in combat there are no passes."

"When was the last time you were in combat, Lieutenant?" asked Ramey.

"Well . . ."

"My point exactly. In a few weeks, we're going to be in the thick of it. Let the troops enjoy themselves now. For some of them, it could be the last time."

"You've heard something?"

Ramey shook his head. "No more than you have. You were there when the general told us that we're going on a great adventure. I think you can figure it out."

"Yes, sir. Anything else?"

"Let's turn all this over to the platoon leaders and then head for the officer's mess. No need for us to work any harder than anyone else."

"Yes, sir." She hesitated and then asked, "You know where it is?"

"Nope. But I plan on learning. If you'll follow me."

"Shouldn't we alert the platoon leaders?"

"Lieutenant, I don't know what's wrong with you." Grinning, he said, "They'll find us if they need us. We don't have to report to them. They have to report to us."

"Yes, sir."

Together they walked down the corridor. Ramey noticed the soldiers, armed with laser rifles, standing guard along it. He knew that their purpose was mainly ceremonial, but felt a chill along his spine. This was what he'd trained for. Combat with a dangerous enemy.

Crowley picked up on it too, but her reaction was different. She laughed and asked, "You think they'll stop the enemy?"

"Nope. But then, I don't think that's the purpose. Just a subtle reminder that a state of war exists."

They reached the mid-lift and Ramey reached out to touch the button. When the door opened he entered and found that the buttons inside were not labeled. There were numbers on them. He had no idea which button to push.

"Now what?" asked Crowley.

Ramey reached out and punched one of the buttons. "We'll have to experiment."

The doors closed gently and he felt the lift begin to move. A moment later the doors opened again and another officer entered. "We're trying to find the officer's mess," Ramey announced.

"Ship's company or infantry?"

"Infantry."

He reached out and hit a button. "Number twenty-seven. Then to the right."

"Thanks."

The doors closed and seemed to open again without movement. Now they faced a different deck. The officer said, "Level twenty-seven."

"Thanks."

They stepped out and joined the crowd. They walked along the corridor and found the officer's mess. Stepping through the hatch, they saw that it was a huge cabin with one end glowing as if it opened into space. In the upper corner at the far end was a bright star. About halfway across the wall was the illuminated disc of a planet, and scattered closer were the ships of the fleet. It was an impressive sight.

Ramey moved toward it and stopped. Only then did he see the rest of the mess. The open expanse of deck was covered with tables and chairs. White linen covered the tables. Only a few of them were occupied.

"Little early for dinner," said Crowley.

"That way we miss the rush." He walked out, took a table in the center and then turned to the holo. "Wonder if it's real time or a recording."

"Probably a recording," said Crowley.

They sat down to wait. Ramey twisted around so that he could watch the fleet for a moment. Then, to Crowley, he said, "This could be real fun."

The conference room was crowded. The highest ranking officers and the regimental commanders sat around the conference table. Their deputies and the battalion commanders occupied the chairs shoved against the bulkheads and set in rows there.

The division commander stood at the head of the table and waited until everyone was seated and ready. That bothered Jefferson because the commander was usually the last to enter the room. He waited until everyone was there and then made a grand entrance.

He was a short, stocky man with gray hair cut short so that it looked like a brush. He had a rounded face, large eyes and a small nose. His hands looked as if they were too big for his body.

"Please," said one of the colonels. "Everyone sit down right now."

Jefferson leaned close to Torrence and said, "This is going to be bad."

The division commander finally ran out of patience. He stood, hands on his hips, and said, "Immediately, we go to a full war footing."

That shut them up. Silence fell like a switch had been thrown. All eyes were on the general as they waited. Jefferson wanted to say something funny to wreck the somber mood but could think of nothing.

"Full war footing means," said the general, "that by this

time next month, we'll be on a planet's surface, either victorious, or in a great deal of trouble. If we're still alive."

"Dramatic," said Jefferson quietly to Torrence.

"Colonel Davis," said the general, "will take over the briefing now."

Davis, an older man, maybe fifty, stood. There was a fringe of white hair around his head. He had gray eyes and a long pointed nose. In his huge hands, he held a sheet of paper that he stared at.

"Thank you, General." He turned slightly. "Intelligence data gathered at great expense in time, effort and in human lives, have provided us with the suspected location of the enemy's home world."

He stopped, waited, but there was no reaction from the assembled officers. He glanced back at the general and shrugged. He wasn't sure what to say.

The general leaned forward. "Ladies and gentlemen. We are about to invade the home world of our enemy, the spacefaring race that attacked us." He searched the faces of those around the table. "We're going after the bastards."

And still no one seemed impressed. The general shrugged and turned his attention to the intelligence officer.

Davis waved a hand and the holo display shimmered, fragmented, and then came together with an almost audible snap.

"This," he said, "is the suspected home world of our enemy."

The holo showed a system with a double star at the center of it. There were planets around only one of the stars. They ranged from small inner planets to gaseous giants that were surrounded by satellites and ring systems.

Again the holo changed, but this time it focused on a single planet. It was a blue, basketball-sized object floating over the center of the table. Clouds obscured part of its surface. Smog hid one coastline. A gray concrete city spread along the banks of a river, reaching down toward the ocean.

"Our recons have been limited," said Davis. "We don't want them to know that we know where they live." He pointed at the planet and added, "But this is it. Size, about one and a half times that of Earth. Atmosphere, standard oxygen-nitrogen, though it is a little oxygen rich. It is an industrial world, though the waste products, smog and atmospheric pollution seem to be limited to a single manufacturing center."

"Why is that?" asked a regimental commander.

Davis shrugged but answered it anyway. "We suspect that most manufacturing takes place on other worlds. They have exported their pollution elsewhere so it won't bother them. They've made their world into a cultural center inhabited only by them. Outsiders are not allowed."

"Racist pigs," said a voice.

Davis turned and grinned. "In every sense of the word. They are only interested in the survival of their species. They will use and discard all others. Their attitude is that they rule—and all other races are inferior."

"Then how in the hell can we expect to defeat them?" asked a battalion commander.

Now the general interrupted. He looked at Jefferson and asked, "Would you care to answer that, General?"

Jefferson glanced at the slowly revolving ball of bright blue and didn't have a clue about what to say. He'd met the enemy twice and had defeated him twice, but the cost had been astronomical. But the problem was that he didn't know how he had been able to beat them. He'd certainly learned of no secret vulnerability.

He ran his hand through his hair and looked at the other officers and had an inspiration. Grinning, he said, "We can beat them because they have never had to fight an enemy on a nearly equal footing. We can win because they don't understand how to fight a war."

Davis nodded and said, "We've found almost no signs of a war fleet. Granted, they have fleets of ships that explore the galaxy, but they have yet to find and then fight another spacefaring race."

Davis stopped and wondered just how far he should go. He wiped a hand over his mouth and then said, "In the mid-1940s, as we first experimented with primitive atomic weapons and launched our first rockets into space, we were visited by flying saucers. I think that those were the first scout craft from this race. We had, you might say, marked our location. They came to look, but we were still confined to the surface of our planet. A surgical strike by them would have crippled us, but they didn't make it. Now, it's too late."

"So why didn't they begin to build a military fleet?" asked one man.

Davis shrugged. "Maybe they didn't understand the concept of war then. Or maybe they did, but they underestimated our ability to develop weapons. Or maybe they believed that they could defeat anything and anyone who came against them. Who knows?"

"Specifics," said the general.

"Yes, sir," said Davis. "They have no standing army. They have no military vessels and in our two encounters with them, we have defeated numerically superior forces." He pointed at the industrial complex. "Targeting will destroy the facilities here. Once they have been neutralized, the invasion can begin."

"Size of the invasion force?" asked Jefferson.

"Our division, two other infantry divisions and the One Hundred Sixteenth Task Group including the newest of our battle fleet."

"Jesus," said a woman.

"Timetable?"

"The first landings are scheduled for one month," said the general.

"Spearhead?" asked Jefferson, suddenly understanding why he had been tapped to command a brigade. It wasn't because they thought he'd done nothing wrong before. It was because he'd fought the enemy twice before. He was the local expert in their tactics.

"Tenth Interplanetary Regiment will land first for interdiction of enemy facilities, disruption of supply lines and destruction of enemy communications capabilities. The remainder of your brigade, General Jefferson, will land within twelve hours with the division to follow within a day."

"Jesus," said Jefferson.

"You can handle it, can't you, General?"

"Yes, sir," said Jefferson. "I'm not thrilled with the idea, though."

"No one asked you for your opinions." The general looked into the faces of the others. "Now you know the outline of the plan. Specific assignments and instructions will be available on the main battle computer."

Davis, who'd let the meeting get away from him, said, "General Jefferson, I'll need to brief you personally on a couple of matters at a later time."

"Certainly," said Jefferson. "Call my aide and have him arrange something."

"Yes, General."

Davis looked at the division commander and said, "That's all I have, sir."

The division CO stood suddenly, indicating the briefing was over. Before he walked out, he said, "In five weeks, I expect to be able to tell the President that the threat has been eliminated."

As he left the conference room, one of the officers said, "Jesus."

3

RAMEY STOOD AT one end of the simulator deck, image enhancer in his hand. The low, rough buildings looked as if they had been constructed of mud and thatch and were tucked in among trees that rose fifty to a hundred feet above the surface. There was no sign of anything modern and there was no sign of life.

Slipping to one knee, he ordered Crowley, "Take one platoon to the south and set up a blocking force. You have fifteen minutes to get into position."

"Radio compliance."

"No radio," said Ramey. "Just get there in fifteen minutes. I'll begin the assault then."

"Yes, sir."

Crowley, bent low, moved along a plastic hedge making sure that her head remained below the level of the plants, tapped the shoulder of a platoon leader and waved him to his feet. The platoon stood without an order from either of them and fanned out behind them.

Ramey watched until they disappeared into the artificial forest of hundred-foot trees. He then turned his attention to the village, searching for some sign that someone was alive in it.

His training had taught him to look for smoke, animals or movement, but he saw nothing. The condition of it seemed too good for it to be abandoned.

Again he dropped down and then turned, sitting on the rough surface of the artificial ground. Heat lamps overhead turned the ship into a sauna. Sweat soaked his uniform and dripped from his face. The body armor, a densely woven shirt, allowed for no air circulation. If they'd been in a cold environment, the shirt would have kept him warm. Now it threatened to kill him.

The first sergeant, an older, stocky man, approached and then knelt. "Everyone is in position for the attack."

"I want the fourth platoon held in reserve just in case," said Ramey. "They can also cover our rear."

"Yes, sir. When do we jump off?"

Ramey looked at his watch. "Seven minutes. Low level assault. We're not going to just open fire and run in. We're got to infiltrate quietly. Let the enemy take the first shot at us."

"Ah . . ."

Ramey grinned. "It's a simulated mission, Sergeant. We'll operate differently in a real combat environment."

"Just checking, sir. One doesn't become an old soldier by letting the enemy have all the advantages."

"I understand."

The sergeant moved off and spread the word to the rest of the troops. The two assault platoons filtered into position, keeping low and out of sight of the village. Ramey, up on his knees again, surveyed it, but there was nothing to see except the seemingly deserted huts.

As the last of the fifteen minutes he'd given Crowley ticked off, he shoved the image enhancer into its case, checked the safety on his laser training aid and then stood. He nodded at the others and took a step forward, pushing his way through the thick plastic of the simulated hedge.

The two platoons joined him and they swept forward, fanning out on line. Glancing right and left, Ramey thought of the videos he'd watched as a kid. The American Army storming the enemy position. Confederate Civil War soldiers attacking up Cemetary Ridge or the Marines crossing the beach of a Pacific island. Now he was leading his troops as they attacked an enemy position.

Ramey forced his mind back on the assault but found it difficult to concentrate. He knew that it wasn't the real thing. He knew that even if the company was wiped out, it would only be on paper and no one would relieve him of his command. They might lecture him on missing the obvious or walking into a trap, but these were training exercises designed so that the commander made the mistakes where it didn't matter.

Fifty yards from the village, Ramey stopped, holding up a hand, his fist closed. The men and women scattered for firing positions as Ramey studied the huts a final time. It looked as deserted as a cemetery at midnight. No sign of life. Ramey knew it was a trap. They wouldn't waste precious simulator time on a fake assault. There was an object lesson to be learned, but Ramey couldn't spot it.

Looking at the second platoon leader, Ramey said, "Pass the word. Only the second platoon. First is to remain here and cover us."

"Dividing the force even more?"

Ramey shrugged. "Better to expose forty troops than eighty. We'll take it slow."

"Yes, sir."

As soon as the word was passed, Ramey was up and moving. He glanced right and left, searching for signs of the ambush that he knew would come. He scanned the fronts of the mud huts, studying the doors and windows. Again he was convinced that there was no attack or ambush. There was nothing to see.

The first of the laser beams stabbed out as the platoon reached the edge of the building. No one saw where it came from. The training harness of one of the men suddenly flashed and buzzed signaling his death. The man sat down on the dusty surface of the simulated ground.

Ramey dropped to one knee. "Anyone see where that came from?" He glanced right and left, searching for the hidden enemy soldiers.

More lasers flashed, but in the bright light of the simulator, it was nearly impossible to see the beams. Training harnesses began to buzz as more of the platoon was "killed."

Ramey shot into the window of a hut, but that did no good. Firing from the unseen enemy increased. He searched for them wildly but couldn't see them.

"Fall back," he ordered.

As he stood to run, he saw a flash out of the corner of his eye. Diving to the right, he rolled to his back and saw an enemy soldier perched in one of the tall trees. The branches and leaves had been arranged to look normal but concealed the firing platforms.

"In the trees," he shouted. "They're in the trees."

At that moment his harness flashed and buzzed and he died a simulated death. But the answer was out. His troops were firing up into the trees. Those of the first platoon were now providing covering fire as the men and women of the second scrambled to get out of the open.

Now the forest around the village erupted with beams. Lasers fired up into the trees, raking them. The flashing and buzzing of training harnesses filled the air.

A moment later, a voice boomed. "Cease firing, Exercise has ended. Cease firing."

Ramey stood and dusted the seat of his pants. He flipped the safety of his weapon to off and waited as the instructors moved out of the trees.

"Caught you with that one, Captain," said an approaching umpire.

"Sure, but the village is now ours."

"If you'd been a little more alert, your casualties would have been fewer. No reason to walk in without checking all the alternatives."

Ramey nodded and thought about holding up advancing troops because a deserted village stood in the way. It was true that he should have been searching the trees too, but the enemy rarely was so good at camouflage that he could hide in the trees without being seen.

"Once the enemy opened fire," said Ramey, "he was trapped. No way to get out of the trees without getting killed."

The umpire shrugged and said, "You don't know that. I make it fourteen killed."

"How many enemy?" asked Ramey.

"Six. That's all there were."

"And you wanted me to hold up the advance because of six enemy soldiers? That could have cost a lot more lives in the long run."

As a company commander, Ramey had a cabin to himself. It was little more than a box, barely six feet on a side, with just enough room for his cot and one chair that kept getting in his way as he tried to move around the cabin. But it was a private room, and that was something that only the highest ranking staff officers rated.

The quiet bong at the door didn't surprise him. He lifted his feet to the deck and stood. He glanced at the towel on the back of the chair but ignored it. He was wearing a T-shirt and shorts.

He opened the hatch and found Crowley standing there. She wore a clean chocolate uniform with red piping and her hair was still shower damp. She glanced at him and asked, "Mind if I come in?"

"Not at all." Ramey turned and pulled the towel from the back of the chair. He looked around and then tossed it on the cot. "Have a seat."

"Thanks." She sat down, crossed her legs carefully and then asked, "You catch any flack over the training exercise this morning?"

Ramey dropped to the cot and said, "No. Tried to berate me for not seeing the enemy in the trees, but I don't think that was valid. It was a trick designed to teach us not to overlook anything obvious." He laughed. "One of our NCOs suggested that I shouldn't have divided the company the way I did without knowing more about the enemy, but hell, it worked."

"Those training exercises are ridiculous," said Crowley. "How often are we going to be fighting an enemy that lives in mud huts and has lasers and the ability to hide in trees like that? Primitives who could conceal themselves that well would be using blow guns or bows and arrows."

Ramey shrugged. "Who knows what we'll find on other

planets? We're dealing with alien intelligence and their racial memories, their abilities, their whole makeup will make them different from us. We just can't guess."

"I can make one guess," said Crowley.

Ramey grinned broadly. "You've been listening to scuttlebutt again."

"Only a little bit and this makes some sense."

"Well?"

"We're not going to be fighting any primitive race that lives in mud huts, and hides in trees. We're going after a spacefaring race. *The* spacefaring race."

"Sure."

"No," said Crowley. "Makes sense. These are the guys that fought them once before. That Jefferson, he's fought them twice. We're on our way now."

"How do you know?"

Crowley shrugged and then said, "First sergeant was talking to a couple of the ship's company. They gave him the straight dope on it."

"Ship's company?"

"Come on, John, the ship's company has to know the destination of the ship. Put that together with what we've heard about Jefferson and it all makes sense."

Ramey stood up and wiped a hand along his jaw. "You know the easiest way to put a stop to the rumors? If you're really worried about them."

"Sure. You call the battalion commander and then the regimental commander. Go right up the chain of command and ask your questions. But what makes you think they'll tell you anything?"

"Because, as a company commander, I have the need to know," said Ramey.

"Right now you don't," said Crowley.

"That's true," said Ramey. He turned and looked down at her. "Aren't you getting terribly uncomfortable in that long, hot uniform?"

For a moment she looked shocked and then said, "It is a little hot in here. I was going to ask you how you could stand it."

Ramey checked the hatch, making sure that it was locked,

and then stood facing her. He reached up and began unbuttoning her tunic. "Why put on all these clothes when you're coming for a visit?"

"Wanted it to look good for the troops. I didn't want to start any more scuttlebutt."

Ramey finished the task and slipped the garment from her shoulders, letting it drop to the deck. Next he attacked the buttons on her shirt, taking it slowly, peeling back the material so that he could see her bare skin.

"It was nice of you not to dress at all," said Crowley.

"No reason to," said Ramey. "I've no roommates to wonder about me."

"You'd think," she said, "that the executive officer would rate a single cabin."

Without answering, Ramey unfastened her belt, unbuttoned and unzipped her pants and pushed them down over her hips. He let them fall to the floor, pooling around her ankles. He reached down and rubbed the inside of her thigh, feeling the soft, smooth skin there. He leaned in close, brushed her lips with his and then nipped at her chin with his teeth.

Crowley kicked her pants free and reached up, putting her hands on his shoulders. She stood there in her underwear, her black uniform socks and black shoes. Ramey took a step back, glanced at her and had to laugh.

"Thanks," she said. "I just love to be undressed by someone and then laughed at by them. Does a hell of a lot for my self-esteem."

"Finish the task," said Ramey, "and I won't be laughing any more. But, you've got to admit that the costume isn't the most erotic ever worn."

Crowley sat down in the chair and took off her shoes and socks. "That better?"

Ramey's voice was suddenly husky. He nodded dumbly and said, "Much."

"The training schedule says that we've an evening formation in about an hour. One or both of us should be there for the morale of the troops. Then one of us should eat at the enlisted mess to make sure that it's up to standards, and we've got an evening inspection on the schedule before lights out. The inspection is fairly routine and I don't think we should make it too tough on them."

"Nothing I like better than discussing the training and inspection schedule with a beautiful woman while we're both in our underwear."

"Oh," she said a little too innocently. "I can fix that." She stood and rolled her panties down her thighs. She kept her eyes on his. "Now I'm not in my underwear."

"If I can get you to forget about the training schedule," he said.

"I only mentioned it so that you'd know how much time we have here."

Ramey took off his shorts and then sat down on the cot. He leaned back and stretched out beside her. "We've got plenty of time."

4

THE ONE THING Jefferson had learned as he'd moved up the chain of command was that more and more time was wasted in staff meetings. A platoon leader knew everyone in his platoon and knew everything that was going on because he was right there with them. A company commander wasn't that far removed, but sometimes the platoons operated as separate units so that briefings and debriefings were required. At the battalion level, with more than a five hundred men and women assigned, the commanding officer might not know everyone, but could probably tell who was and who wasn't assigned to his or her battalion. He needed staff meetings and briefings so that he knew what each of the companies in the battalion was doing.

At the regimental level, with four or five battalions, it was nearly impossible to know everyone, and because the functions of battalions differed from one to the next, the CO had to have meetings two or three times a week so that he knew what was happening in each battalion.

Now, at brigade, with three regiments made up of newcomers, Jefferson had no clue as to who they were or what they could do. Too much to keep track of. He had staff officers and assistant staff officers filling a variety of roles. There were staff officers who took care of weapons, who made sure the troops were fed, that their taxes were filed and paid, that they voted in hometown and home planet elections, that they had high morale and that their exploits were printed and videoed for the hometown folks. There were staff officers for jobs that he'd never heard of, and most of them were field grade, meaning they were majors or above.

So, with the whole staff assembled, crowded around the conference table that had held more than enough places when he was a lowly regimental commander, Jefferson was getting bored. No one had told him that the staff officers, with almost no chance for glory would tell everyone at the staff meetings everything about his or her job. In great detail. As if there were nothing more important in the entire universe.

Jefferson had lost track of what was being discussed. He glanced down at the computer screen concealed below the level of the table. Only he could see it. Regimental commanders and his executive officer also had screens, just in case something happened that required their attention.

The cursor on the screen blinked red, signaling that there was an important message. Jefferson reached down and touched a key. The message began parading across the screen. "This is ridiculous. We don't need this detail." The initials that followed were "V.T."

Jefferson looked up at the man speaking and suddenly broke in. "Thank you, Major."

"But, General, I haven't touched on the . . ."

"Thank you anyway, Major. There is much to cover today and we seem to be getting bogged down."

The man looked crushed but nodded and sat down. Before anyone else could stand, Jefferson held up a hand. "Ladies and gentlemen, I know that each of you has pressing duties, and I think we've taken enough of your time for today. Those who feel that they have a problem they can't handle by themselves, I'll be in my office."

With that he stood and headed for the hatch. There was a babble of conversation behind him, but he didn't stop or turn.

To do so would be to invite them to ask questions and seek his advice. It would take an hour to break free.

He dived out the hatch, heard it iris shut behind him and then fell back against the bulkhead. He felt as if he'd just escaped from the enemy.

"Not all of us are fooled by the bluster," said Torrence.

Jefferson opened his eyes and then shook his head. "It was difficult enough to run a regiment. Now I've got a brigade. I don't want to get caught in those meetings. They accomplish nothing and the staff officers think it's the only time they have to perform. They're in there bucking for their promotions and advancements."

The hatch began to iris again. Jefferson glanced at it and said, "Let's get out of here."

"Yes, General. Don't you think the others will get annoyed with you playing favorites?"

"Let them," said Jefferson. "Serve them right."

They reached the stern-lift and waited for it. Looking at Torrence, he asked, "Where did they find them?"

"Earth. In the fleet. Scattered around and now with all the slots that were open, they were scrambling for people to fill them."

"Thanks for reminding me," said Jefferson.

"You're not going to play that same sad song again?" asked Torrence.

For an instant Jefferson felt a flare of anger, but it burned out rapidly. Torrence was the only officer in his command who could get away with such a comment, and that was because she'd been on the planet with him when the Tenth Interplanetary Infantry had ceased to exist.

The lift hatch opened and they entered. Jefferson hesitated before touching the buttons. He wasn't sure where he wanted to go or what he had to do.

"I need to get to my headquarters," said Torrence.

"Let's go to mine first," he said.

"Anything important going on?" she asked.

Jefferson hit the button and felt the lift move. To her, he said, "No, not really."

"Fine."

They rode in silence for several seconds and then the lift stopped. As the hatch opened, Torrence hesitated, letting Jefferson step out first. There was an opulence to that end of the ship. It was where the generals lived and worked and extra time, effort and money had been spent to make sure that the generals had as much comfort as they could stand.

They walked down the corridor. The cabins on the right and left were filled with people working hard. Clerks and aides and staff officers hurried to finish complex tasks. There was the clacking of keyboards, the hum of disks, and the hammering of printers.

They reached Jefferson's office. His secretary came to attention, as did his aide. Neither of them said a word as Jefferson walked through to his office.

As they entered, Torrence turned slowly, as if inspecting it. "Much better than mine."

"We generals have to have big offices. It's in the manual, somewhere."

"Lot of wasted space. We are, after all, on a spaceship."

"Sit down, Vicki, and stop trying to pick a fight with me."

"Yes, General."

Jefferson slipped into his chair and touched a couple of buttons. The outside bulkhead seemed to fall away giving them a view of space.

"Real time?" asked Torrence.

"Yeah. Fleet will be fragmenting in the next few days. Our brigade will split off, as will the other two brigades. We rendezvous in a month, just after we begin the assault."

"I've been wondering about that," said Torrence.

"That's one of the reasons I'm glad you're here now. Your regiment will drop in about twelve hours early to interdict the enemy's lines of communication."

"Now why am I not surprised?"

"We've interrogated the people we freed on other planets. The captives held by these . . . grays. They tell us that there are humans still being held on Zeta Reticuli. It's one of the reasons, the main reason, we can't just stand off, out in space,

and drop bombs." Jefferson turned so that he was staring at the fleet. He didn't want to look at her. "Orders from the division commander say we have to land and attempt to free those people before the main assault."

"And you can get them changed," she said. "If you wanted to do it."

Now Jefferson did look at her. "You want them changed, you got it. I let them stand because I think you've got the best chance of getting in and doing the job and bringing out those people while the majority of your regiment survives. That's my thinking."

"Thanks," she said somewhat sarcastically. "But I don't know these kids."

"You watch the exercise this afternoon?" asked Jefferson.

"You mean with that wise-guy captain, what's his name? Ramey?"

"That's the one," said Jefferson. "He seemed to know his business. That trick usually takes out more than a squad when it's pulled. That suggests that not all of your new people are useless."

"So he got lucky," said Torrence.

"He's one of your people, Vicki. You want to think of it as luck, then go ahead."

Torrence stood up and walked to the bulkhead. It looked as if she was about to step out into space. With her hands on her hips, she studied the fleet.

"I think I'm beginning to understand what you must feel," Torrence said. "I watched that kid operate and all I could think about was how the moves he made would get him killed and it would be my fault. All I could see were the rows of black body bags waiting for shipment or burial."

"Except in that situation, he made the best moves possible," said Jefferson.

Now she turned and looked at him. "You seem to have gotten over your depression."

"That's unfair," said Jefferson.

"Yeah. I know." She jammed her hands in her pockets and studied the deck. "I haven't even lost anyone yet and I know what you were going through. I could stand here, we all could, and talk about how it wasn't your fault the regiment got chopped up, but that doesn't make it easier, does it?"

"Rationalizations never help," Jefferson said quietly. "I wonder if I wasn't given command of this brigade and this assignment because you know, just know, it's going to be rough on us. Maybe they figure I'll get killed and that will resolve the problem."

"Which means that the men and women of the brigade aren't important," she said. Then, shaking her head, she added, "I think you've got it because you always manage to win. The losses might be high, but you win, and in this one, victory is all that counts."

Jefferson took a deep breath and exhaled slowly. "Vicki, I don't like this. I don't want to order anyone else into battle. Not into this battle. I just can't do it anymore."

"You have to and now I have to." She lifted her eyes and stared at him. "And there is nothing we can do about it." She was silent for a moment. "I remember a video from long ago. The soldier, knowing that the battle was about to be fought wanted to know why. And the old sergeant said, 'Because we're here and nobody else.' So we've got to do this because there is nobody else."

Jefferson leaned forward and propped an elbow on his desk. "Nobody else."

"So I'm going in first," she said.

"Tactic plans haven't been finalized yet," said Jefferson, "but I trust you to do the job right. And I don't suppose I need remind you that everything we've just discussed is classified at the highest level."

"No, you don't have to remind me. And yes, I'll do the best I can," said Torrence.

"We'll have a full-scale briefing in the next few hours. Division commander wants to meet with all brigade and regimental commanders before the fleet fragments."

"So how long do we have?" she asked.

"Three hours," said Jefferson.

She pointed at the hatch and asked, "Does that lock?"

"Of course. But then, I tell my aide that I don't want to be disturbed for any reason and it's the same thing."

"You tell him that and he's going to figure out what we're doing. You quietly lock the hatch and he won't be any the wiser unless he tried to enter." She moved away from the bulkhead and sat down on the couch. She took off her shoes and then her socks. "You're not moving."

"I'm a little bothered by this situation," said Jefferson.

"Why? It's not like we've never done this before."

"No, but that was before I became the brigade commander."

"You were the regimental commander and I was your exec. The situation has changed for the better."

"You're still in my chain of command."

"But," she said standing so that she could slip out of her pants, "I'm now a regimental commander with my own chain of command. It's different than it was. You're not feeling guilty, are you?"

Jefferson didn't speak for a moment. The thoughts were coming too fast. Guilt wasn't quite the right word. He was worried about how it would look to the outsiders. He was worried about what the division commander would think. He was worried how the other regimental commanders would react if they knew the whole story.

"No, not guilty," he said. "Cautious."

"Well, cautious I can handle." She stripped her tunic and dropped it on the couch. "You know, we don't have many opportunities to take a little pleasure for ourselves. When we get one, we shouldn't waste it worrying about trivia."

Jefferson nodded, but said, "I'll only say this once. The way things are, I think it has to be said."

"I don't like the tone here." She was standing in her underwear, looking first at Jefferson and then out at the fleet.

"You don't have to do this. . . ."

"Oh, Jesus, David, what in the hell is wrong with you? I'm the one who's standing here practically naked and you're worried about forcing me into something I don't want to do. Jesus! Get with the program."

"I just wanted to say that for the record." He stood and asked, "You want me to blank the bulkhead?"

"They can't see in here, can they?"

"Nope."

"Then leave it. It'll be like doing it outside."

5

COMMODORE JACK CLEMENS sat on the bridge of his flagship, a new Saturn class battle cruiser, and watched as the sailors did their jobs. Clemens, who had survived the disaster that had all but wiped out Jefferson's regiment, was an older man with graying hair and dark brown eyes. He had a pointed nose, narrow features, and a long, almost graceful neck.

"Scout ship approaching," said one of the sailors.

"Put it up on the main screen," said Clemens.

"We're at the extreme end of the magnification scale," said the sailor. "On center screen."

Clemens turned his attention to it. On his old ship, it would have been little more than a speck. A gray dot that was ill defined and unrecognizable. Now it was a black ship, small, with the fins obvious.

"Time to intercept?" asked Clemens.

"Twenty minutes."

"You have an ID on him?"

"Yes, Captain. He's transmitted the IFF code. It's probably Kit Carson."

"They're all called Kit Carson," said Clemens. "Kind of a tradition."

"Aye, sir."

Clemens pushed himself out of the captain's chair and took a single step forward. "I'll be in the shuttle bay when he arrives. If there is a deviation in his course, or an incoming message, you alert me immediately."

"Aye, aye. Captain."

Clemens left the bridge, letting the sailors go back to work. It was a new crew but a good one. They hadn't seen any action, but they had been so well trained that they would do their jobs as the bridge burned around them or all the air was sucked into space.

Clemens hurried down the corridor to the mid-lift and rode it to another corridor. He walked along it and then entered the control room overlooking the shuttle bay.

As he walked in, one of the controllers turned and said, "Be about fifteen minutes, Captain."

"Any communication with the pilot?"

"Just the routine."

Clemens moved forward so that he could look out into the shuttle bay. There was a single shuttle, squatting on its legs, and two scout craft. Technicians crawled over one of them, preparing it for flight as the scout stood off to one side watching their every move.

A few minutes later, a klaxon sounded and the technicians deserted their stations. Once they were clear of the bay, a red light came on, warning everyone that the air was being pumped out so that an incoming ship could dock.

Clemens watched the approach of the scout ship on one of the monitors. Lights in the shuttle bay were extinguished except for those used to guide the scout craft. A line of alternating green and red lines blinked, marking the center line of the shuttle bay.

Blast shutters dropped into place in front of the glass of the control room. Although the glass was strong enough to withstand a direct hit from a laser and had a self-sealing capability, no one wanted to take a chance.

"He's about one minute out. Opening outer doors."

Now Clemens could easily see the shape of the one-man scout craft. It was a bullet-shaped ship with fins in the rear and a bubble canopy on the top. There was a hatch on one side that allowed access for the pilot.

The scout seemed to race toward the side of the ship, slowed, and then hovered for a moment. It began to inch forward until the nose penetrated the main outer doors. It slipped lower and then pushed its way in. As it contacted the deck the outer doors were closed.

"Pumping air back in."

The red lights continued to flash, dimmed and then went out, replaced by green.

"It's safe to enter, Captain."

Clemens nodded and left the control room. He entered the shuttle bay as the technicians were working to get the scout out of his ship.

Looking at the side of it, he said, "What's that scorching along there?"

"Could be a laser," said one of the men, shrugging. He bent to look closer.

"Could be from bouncing along the atmosphere," said one of the women.

They opened the hatch and one of the men crouched and looked up into the craft. He reached out with his right hand. A pair of feet, in sandals, appeared, followed by legs and then a waist. When the feet contacted the deck, the technicians moved back out of the way.

The scout ducked down and stepped away from the hatch. He was a short, thin man with almost no hair on his head, but he had a thick beard. It looked as if he'd put all the effort into growing the beard. He saluted Clemens and said, "Permission to come aboard, sir."

"Permission granted."

"Thank you."

"You want something to eat or drink?"

"Cup of coffee would be nice," said the scout. "A Coke would be better."

"While the technicians clear your cameras, sensors and recorders, we'll find you something to eat and drink."

"And a shower."

Clemens couldn't help laughing. "Yeah. A shower."

* * *

Sitting in the conference room, the scout, now wearing a clean flight suit and no shoes, was sipping a Coke. The bulkhead was gone, replaced by a view of the enemy's home world as the tapes and films were projected through the holo.

"That's their home planet," said Kit Carson, pointing at the holo.

Clemens had seen tapes of it before. There didn't seem to be anything new on this tape.

The view changed abruptly. "That's the main city. The industrial complex."

"Any sign of defenses?"

"Yes, sir."

That wasn't the answer that Clemens had expected. Everything he'd heard from all the previous reports was that there were no defensive weapons anywhere.

"What happened?"

"I was scanned as I entered orbit around the planet. Momentary scans and I couldn't tell if they were just routine radars and sensors, or if they'd spotted me and were checking me out."

"That's passive," said Clemens, "and doesn't suggest any type of defensive areas."

"You saw the scorch marks on the side of my ship. That was from ground defenses," said Carson.

"What type of defenses?"

"Well," said Carson, sipping his Coke and keeping his eyes on the photos being displayed, "looks like some primitive lasers. They didn't have the power or the range to harm me or my ship. We just breezed in and out."

"Of course," said Clemens, "that tells them something about our capabilities."

"Yes, sir. But they've already faced us twice. I don't think there was anything they learned from my survey that they didn't already know."

Clemens turned to the right and touched the computer keyboard. He asked if he could get a look at the locations of the enemy defensive installations with a coding that would tell him which were new.

The scene on the holo changed slowly, drifting into swirling colors and then solidifying. Now he had a good view of the enemy's industrial complex as seen from a hundred thousand feet. Lights flashed around it, making it look like a Christmas decoration.

"They've been busy," said Clemens.

"I only observed laser facilities and it seems that our shielding is a good defense against them."

"Invasion pods will be vulnerable," said Clemens.

Carson drained his Coke and set the can on the table. He turned and then stood, walking toward the representation of the enemy's industrial complex. He studied the flashing lights that marked the enemy's suspected laser defenses and then said, "There are other facilities that looked new to me but I couldn't tell what they were. They could be weapons or they could just be new structures for manufacturing. Hell, they could be anything at all."

"We'll need to target all those."

Carson turned and looked at Clemens. "I hope there were other scout missions."

"We held them down," said Clemens, "because we didn't want to tip our hand."

"They've got to know that we're coming," Carson said. "We aren't fooling anyone."

"I know. That's what frightens me."

Carson, having finished his meal, taken another shower, and dressed in another clean uniform, was back in the shuttle bay. He walked around his ship, checking the outside of it, searching for damage done by the enemy defenses or by the microscopic debris that littered space.

The paint on his ship was pitted slightly on the sides and had begun to corrode along the nose. The scorch marks had dulled the finish even more than normal, but Carson didn't mind that. Bright, shiny paint was something that only those who didn't understand the requirements of stealth demanded. Dull paint was harder to see. The scorch marks actually enhanced the stealth capabilities.

One of the technicians approached, hooked an electrical

cable to the ship and then stepped to the side. To Carson, he said, "Boy, I sure don't envy you boys in the scouts."

Carson rubbed his chin and asked, "Why not?"

"All that time alone in space. No one around to talk to. Having to rely on your own abilities."

"Don't have to put up with all the bullshit," said Carson. "And I'd rather trust my life to me than some guy sitting on the bridge. I make a mistake and get killed, then that's my own tough luck. Guy on the bridge makes a mistake and I get killed, then it's his tough luck. Nothing I can do there."

"If something goes wrong, there's no one out there to help you."

"But then if something goes wrong on your ship, there's no one around to help you either."

"I have a better chance to survive. There are a lot of other people around. On the ship."

Carson shrugged. "So you believe, but I'd rather rely on myself than a bunch of strangers." Carson looked at the man. "How old are you anyway?"

"Nineteen. Why?"

"Well, no offense," said Carson, "but I trust myself to get me out of bad situations more than I would trust a bunch of teenagers."

"I know my job," said the man.

"And I have no quarrel with that. I'm just saying that I trust my judgment more than I trust yours, or for that matter, the captain's."

"Still, it must get lonely."

"I've got a computer system, I've got video, and I've got radio. I have to navigate and I have to watch for the enemy. There's plenty to do. I don't have time to get lonely."

"But . . ."

"Look, kid, I'm my own commander. I can get away with modifications to the uniform that you'd never even think of. I can wear a beard if I want and blame it on the lack of shaving facility. I'm given a mission and a time frame and then left on my own to do it. And if I'm late, they don't scream at me for that. They ask me what happened."

"Yes, sir." The technician retreated then.

Carson opened the hatch, ducked and stood on the deck, his head up into the cockpit. The lights were all on because the external power unit hooked into his ship. He reached up, touched a couple of test switches and saw that everything was working properly. He twisted around and checked the video tapes near his left side. They were all the same tapes that he'd had on the previous trip. No one had exchanged them with the library on the ship.

Satisfied that all systems were still operating, Carson ducked again. As he stood up, he saw Clemens coming across the deck at him.

"Whenever the ship's captain comes down to visit," said Carson, "it's bad news."

"Not bad," said Clemens. "Just that you're going to have to head over to a different ship. You're to join Jefferson's brigade."

"Thought that was here."

"Nope," said Clemens. "At the moment I'm attached to the division but not part of Jefferson's brigade. Maybe later."

"How soon?"

"Whenever," said Clemens. "I didn't get the impression that it was something that had to be accomplished right this minute."

"How far away are they?"

"Half an AU," said Clemens. "At the moment the whole division is pretty much together here. We're just beginning to fragment as we make the run for the enemy."

"Half an AU is barely an afternoon's flight. Hell, just a couple of hours at most," said Carson. "Guess I'll make the hop just as soon as I can get ready."

"You're welcome to spend the next twenty-four hours here. I can put copies of the tapes and readings on a probe. It'll be there for them in what, two hours."

"I'll take it over," said Carson. "That's actually part of my job."

"Suit yourself," said Clemens.

"Thanks for your hospitality, Captain."

"Any time. Please let me know when you're ready to take off again."

"Yes, sir."

Carson watched Clemens walk across the deck, stop at the hatch and let its iris open. He then glanced at the technician who was dragging a yellow cart toward the ship. Carson wanted to tell him that this was the reason he was a scout. The ship's captain hadn't ordered him to make the trip. Gave him the information and then let Carson decide what he wanted to do. That was the sort of independence that he craved.

"Be ready in about twenty minutes," said the technician.

"I'll be back then. Want to trade some tapes with the library."

"Aye, sir. I'll have everything set for you."

"Thanks."

6

THE FLEET HAD fragmented, with the ships of Jefferson's brigade breaking away from the main fleet and the rest of the division, and then heading straight for the Zeta Reticuli system. The remainder of the division, along with the supporting units, was taking a longer course that would bring it into the fight ten to twelve hours after the initial drop by Jefferson's three regiments.

Now the fleet was scattered through space, some of the vessels separated by more than an astronomical unit. The picket ships, small craft that raced around the edges of the main fleet, were searching for signs that the enemy was approaching. If that happened, the fleet would draw together so that each of the vessels would have the support of all the others.

But at the moment, more than ten light years from the Zeti Reticuli system, no one was concerned about the enemy. Most were more frightened by the training schedule that loomed in front of them. It looked as if it had been designed by monsters just to make the life of the troopers as miserable as possible. No one was thinking about the bigger picture, when they would be dropped onto a planet's surface. Now they just wanted to survive the training being thrown at them.

Corporal Bill Cooper sat on the rough surface in the simulator, sweat soaking his uniform, and listened to the sounds around him. He could easily hear the scrap of feet against the simulated stone as part of his squad tried to climb an outcropping to emplace a machine-gun. Cooper had been helping them, but as they got higher, room to maneuver had diminished and the only course he could follow was to slip down and out of the way.

Cooper was a young man, having just turned twenty. He had dropped out of school and had no prospects for a good job on Earth, so he had joined the Army. When he did, he didn't know that a war was about to erupt. He'd seen the Army as a way of improving his life when he returned to Earth. Now he wondered if that was ever going to happen.

He took out his canteen and sipped at the water, telling himself that he only should take a mouthful. The water had to last for the duration of the exercise and each of them had been given only a single canteen. The point was to teach them discipline.

Cooper capped the canteen and slid it back into the holder. He stood and stepped to the right and then climbed up on the hot rock. He found a place where he could look over the top but there was nothing to see. Just a forest of short trees fashioned from plastic. There were noises in it, but they sounded like animals. Of course they were animals that had never lived on the Earth.

Turning, he looked up at the machine-gun crew. "How's it going?"

"Ten minutes."

"You're behind schedule," said Cooper. "Rest of the platoon is probably set."

"That's not our problem," said one man. "You could help, you know."

"Not my job. I'm now a supervisor. I tell you where to put it and when you're required to put it there."

"Thanks."

A sergeant appeared and looked up at the machine-gun crew. She turned to Cooper. "What's the holdup here?"

"Just getting it in place. It's a little awkward."

"I don't want to hear about it," she said. "I want that gun ready in the next five minutes."

"We'll do our best," said Cooper.

"Get it done." She whirled and rushed off.

Cooper crawled up the rock and slipped around to the right. The field of fire was good but cover was lacking. They were going to be exposed up there.

"I hope that we'll only be supporting an attack and not trying to repel the enemy."

"Just get the damned thing set."

"Yes, sir," said a man sarcastically.

Now the platoon leader appeared. He stopped, looked up at the machine-gun and said, "That's not the best position for it."

"But it gives us the best view of the approaches. We've good fields of fire."

"But the crew is exposed."

"Yes, sir."

"Move it to the right where the crew will have some cover. I don't want to throw away a machine-gun crew."

"Yes, sir."

The platoon leader disappeared. Cooper slipped down the rock and then said, "You heard him."

"Christ, that's all we need."

Cooper crawled up on the rock and then dropped back down. There was nothing for him to do except get in the way. He stood at the base of the rock and watched as the machine-gunner and his assistant struggled to get the weapon down.

When they were on the ground, Cooper said, "Let's set it up at the base of the rock here. Provides some protection."

"No. Richochets off the rock could take us out. I want to be over there, at the edge of the trees. Gives us cover from above and behind and there's something for the incoming rounds to hit besides us."

"You've got an obstruction right here."

"Put a fireteam here," said the machine-gunner. "They can cover our flank."

Cooper looked at the area and then nodded. "I'll get with the squad leader."

"Better hurry."

Cooper pushed his way through the light forest and then heard a sudden, rising shout. He whirled as the enemy appeared at the top of the rock he'd just left. They were firing down at the machine-gunner and his assistant, both of whom had been simulated-killed immediately. The enemy grabbed the weapon, turned it, and opened fire on the forest, hosing down the trees.

From his vantage point, Cooper could tell that it wasn't a well-coordinated assault. The enemy was swarming, killing everything that moved, grabbing weapons and firing blind. They were attacking like an undisciplined mob, but sometimes that was all it took. A mob with enough determination and enough numbers.

Then one of the enemy spotted Cooper, shouted, and all of them began to run toward him. Cooper held his ground for a moment, realized that he could do nothing about the enemy, and then turned to sprint away.

"Based on the information brought by Carson," said Torrence, "I plan to drop from one hundred thousand feet, free fall to five thousand and deploy on the edges of the industrial area. Platoon- and company-sized raids on the aerial defenses before attacking lines of communications. At the same time, we'll be working our way forward to free the prisoners."

Torrence turned and looked at the officers assembled in the briefing room. She was standing on a slightly raised stage with the holo display of the enemy's industrial complex floating in space behind her.

In front of her were rows of plush seats. Jefferson and two of his staff were sitting in the front row. The four battalion commanders and the sixteen company commanders of her regiment were spread out behind them.

"Special assignments will be determined in the next few days and then special training will be arranged for those units." She glanced at Jefferson and then at the officers behind him. "Are there any questions?"

One of the commanders stood. "How will the assignments be determined?"

"You are?" asked Torrence.

Jefferson turned and looked over his shoulder at the man standing there.

"James Reston, captain, commanding Company C of the Third Battalion."

"Well, Captain," said Torrence.

Jefferson stood up and said, "If I may, Colonel."

"Certainly, General."

Jefferson turned to address the man. "First, our problem is that we just don't know much about most of the people assigned to the regiment and the brigade. Almost everyone is new. We'll be evaluating everyone through the exercises."

"Seems to me," said Reston, "that exercises aren't the best way of evaluating a soldier's ability in combat."

"True," said Jefferson, "but at the moment that's all we have." He stared at the soldier. "There are enough assignments that everyone will have one."

"Yes, General."

As Reston sat down, Jefferson addressed the rest of the regiment. "I want everyone to understand one thing here. This is not a contest where there will be some kind of prize at the end." He shook his head. "We're talking about an attack on an enemy who has the weapons to make that attack costly."

He looked at them, watching each of them. "You know, there is nothing glorious about war. There is only death. I don't understand the fascination with war, the desire to get into the fight, and the continual striving to get back into battle."

"It's something we have to do," said one of the company commanders.

"There is no doubt that we have to fight this war. The enemy has made it perfectly clear. But we don't have to look forward to the fight, and we don't have to try to get the so-called plum assignments."

Now Jefferson turned and looked at Torrence standing on the stage. "Sorry, Colonel. I didn't mean to climb up on my soap box."

"That's fine, General. Are there any other questions?"

No one wanted to ask anything. They stared at the holo, at the swirling clouds and the shifting shadows of the enemy's industrial city.

Torrence looked at her officers and then said, "I think that there are those of you who don't believe that we should land and invade on the ground. I'm sure that there are those of you who believe we should attack from space, eliminate the enemy's war-making ability on the ground before we send in the troops. But there are human beings held captive on that planet."

She stopped talking and tried to look into their faces. It wasn't very bright in the room, making it hard for her to see her officers. But she knew she had their attention.

"We have with us a woman who was captured, from Earth, by these beings. I'm going to let her talk to you." Torrence turned to the right and said, "Cynthia?"

A small slender woman with short red hair walked to the podium. She wore a one-piece flight suit that looked to be a size or two too large for her. As she reached the center of the stage, she sniffed once and then rubbed her eye with her index finger. Her skin was so white that it looked unnatural.

She stood there looking out at the soldiers, but she didn't say a word. Torrence finally broke the silence. "Go ahead."

"I was born and raised in Minnesota," she said. "Until I was eighteen. And then they came." She pointed behind her at the bulkhead, but there was nothing there to indicate what she meant.

"Landed at night and took me as I walked in the woods behind the house. Took me away. Into their ship and then to their world. Nothing I could do."

"Tell us about the captivity," Torrence said gently.

Cynthia looked at Torrence and nodded. "They have a building in the center of their city. We lived in cells below the surface. One person to a cell and almost no chance to talk to anyone. Just brought out to work. All day long. Whatever they wanted done. Then back into the cells. If you talked, you were beaten."

"Sounds primitive," said one of the officers.

Cynthia shot a glance at the officers. "They didn't waste much on us. We were their slaves who lived at their whim. Worse than criminals in prison. There, the prisoner has some hope of freedom. Parole and the end of the sentence. We had nothing like that."

"You got free," said an officer.

"I don't understand it," she said. "When I was taken, we didn't travel through space. Oh, sure, we'd landed on the moon and put one expedition on Mars, but that's not real space travel. I didn't know that we could, so there was no hope. Besides, I hadn't done anything to deserve that fate. Nothing at all."

"How'd you get free?"

"They moved me from their home to another planet and then you came. If it hadn't been for you, I'd still be there. Or I'd be dead."

Torrence moved to the center of the stage and put a hand on Cynthia's shoulder. The woman jumped and then settled down. She glanced at Torrence and tried to smile.

"That's all we need," said Torrence. "You can head back to your quarters if you'd like."

"Certainly." She started to turn and then stopped. She looked at the assembled officers and said, "If you can't free the people, kill them."

As Cynthia walked from the stage, Torrence took her place and asked, "Any comments?" She waited for a moment, letting the information settle in. Finally she said, "If not, then you're dismissed to rejoin your units. I'll be in my office for the next hour if anyone needs to talk to me."

Jefferson got to his feet and someone yelled, "Ladies and gentleman, the general."

Before he could move, Torrence said, "General, I'd like to speak with you for a moment."

"I'll meet you in your office, Colonel."

"Yes, General."

With that, Jefferson left the briefing room, stopping in the corridor outside it. To Carter, he said, "Is it me or does it seem that the officers are getting younger all the time?" Jefferson was ignoring the story he'd just heard. He didn't want to think about it.

"Must be you, General. How old are you now?"

Jefferson looked at his intelligence officer and was thankful that Carter let the subject of the captive go. For an instant, he was confused and then understood the question. Because of the medal and his involvement in a half-dozen conflicts, Jefferson was one of the youngest men ever to rise to flag rank. The officers in the briefing room, if they weren't older than he was, were at the most a year or two younger.

"I guess it just seems they're younger."

"Yes, General."

Torrence joined him a moment later. "My office?"

"I suspect," said Jefferson, "that as a general, I shouldn't agree to that. I think you should have to come to mine."

"Yours is farther."

"That's true," said Jefferson. He glanced at Carter and the other officer. "You're free to return to headquarters."

"Don't you want to talk with Carson before he goes out again?" asked Carter.

"Of course. See to it that he doesn't leave before then."

"Yes, sir."

As Carter left, Jefferson turned to Torrence. "What can I do for you?"

She grinned at him shyly. "Let's talk in my office."

"Lead on."

They walked down the corridor which was not guarded by armed soldiers. Jefferson had never liked the idea, and when his brigade had broken away from the main division, he had ordered a suspension of the guards.

They reached Torrence's office. Jefferson recognized it, and then knew that he couldn't have. His office had been on one of the ships that Clemens had lost during the battle. It was a duplicate of it, but it was not quite the same.

Torrence sat down behind the desk and touched the keyboard of the computer to let it know she was there. She glanced at the messages on the screen and then decided that she'd better ignore them because the general was with her.

"Sorry, General," she said.

Jefferson had slipped into the only other chair and said, "If it was anyone but you, I'd be annoyed. But we've worked together for too long."

"Thanks," she said. She turned and looked at him squarely. "I've got to say that I'm uncomfortable now."

"Because I'm a general?" asked Jefferson.

"No. Because I'm a regimental commander. It doesn't feel right."

"This is one hell of a time to tell me," said Jefferson. "Especially after all the things you've said to me in the recent past."

She shrugged. "Well, in the briefing just now, you had to come to my rescue."

"I didn't think of it that way. There were things that I wanted to say, that's all. I probably shouldn't have said anything. It wasn't my place."

"You're the general."

"But it's your regiment."

"When you sat in this chair, did you feel . . . ? Were you sure that . . . ?"

"Come on, Vicki, you know what I thought. I relied on you to pull me through. Hell, you should have been the commanding officer before I was. You were ready then. All I had was the damned medal."

She rocked back. "I didn't fully understand. Not until I realized that I was going to be selecting the specific targets and which units would attack them. People's lives are in my hands."

"So you have to think things through," said Jefferson. He stared at her and wondered if she wasn't saying these things because of his feelings that he should be on a prison ship rather than promoted.

She turned so that she was looking down at the computer screen, but she didn't see the information scrolling across it. "Sometimes, I guess, we each need to be reassured. I wanted to know that you believed I could do the job."

"Yeah," said Jefferson. "I know you can. In fact, you might be better at my job than I am."

"No, I'll let you have the headaches for three regiments. I have enough trouble with my one. Any advice on selecting which units to hit which targets?"

"You should never be afraid to stack the deck in your favor," said Jefferson. "Use as much mechanical equipment as you can. Never use a foot soldier when a robot or bomb will do the job. Lives should be protected whenever possible. It takes twenty years to replace a soldier, but it only takes a few weeks to replace equipment."

"Okay," she said.

Jefferson looked at her. "There something else?"

"No, not really. Well, yes, I guess so. I know that all this is new, your promotion and mine, but I wondered what it was going to do to us."

"I wouldn't think anything," said Jefferson.

"Before, you and I worked together in the same office. Now . . ."

"Hell, we're on the same ship. It's not like I've moved to another division."

"I guess."

Jefferson stood up, suddenly uncomfortable himself. "We'll be okay," he said. "We'll still be . . . it will still be like it was. It's just that I've got so many more responsibilities, as do you."

"Tonight then," she said.

"After all the work is finished, fine." He moved to the hatch.

"You're sure we're okay?"

"Yes, Vicki. We're fine. Tonight."

"I'll be looking forward to it."

7

THE SIMULATOR SHIP was dark, the only light coming from the few overhead lights had been turned down so that they resembled stars. The interior of the ship had been changed so that it resembled the aerial photos of the enemy's industrial city. And set prominently in the center of the deck was a defensive complex constructed so that it looked like those identified in the pictures.

The interior design was based solely on the information provided by Jefferson, the survivors of his regiment, and comments made by the freed prisoners during a few declassified debriefings. They had all told the designers what they had seen of enemy weapons systems and how they had built on the planets where they had been discovered. There was no intelligence data as to what was inside the defensive complex or how they were guarded. It was a creation designed to test the abilities of the soldiers.

Jefferson and Torrence sat together in the umpire's shack with half a dozen monitors in front of them. Each screen picked up a portion of the complex, enhanced the available light, and then using computers, displayed the scene as if it was seen at high noon on a bright day.

Steven Garvey, the video journalist, sat in a chair behind them, his camera set up so he could record the training exercise directly. He was sitting back, enjoying himself because he wasn't involved in the training. He was happy to be sitting down and watching the others work.

Jefferson leaned close to Torrence, glanced back at Garvey to make sure the reporter couldn't hear, and whispered, "One surprise. This will be the final rehearsal."

"What?"

"We're getting very close. After tonight, we get everything ready for the drop."

Torrence took a deep breath and then nodded. "Good. The troops were beginning to get a little worried. They're itching for action."

"Yeah," said Jefferson, though he understood. It wasn't as if they wanted to get into the fight, or start the battle, it was that they wanted to get it over. And the sooner the better. They'd spent weeks in space heading into the fight. They knew it was coming and that there would be no last-minute reprieve. The battle would be fought. Therefore, they wanted to get it over with. The danger, a deadly danger, was in front of them.

Garvey leaned forward and tapped Jefferson on the shoulder. "What are you two whispering about?"

"Nothing," said Jefferson.

"Okay," said Torrence, pointing at one of the screens. "Here they come." She knew that Garvey's attention would now be diverted to the screens.

Ramey lay at the very edge of the defensive position and tried to see the small map he had been given. There wasn't much detail on it. Faint lines glowed on the map, showing him the best attack routes and the lines of retreat.

Spread out on either side of him was his company, waiting for him to make a move or initiate the attack. He hesitated for a moment longer and then slowly climbed to his feet.

Without glancing in either direction, he began to run across the open ground, heading for what appeared to be a chain-link fence. Before reaching it, he threw himself to the ground and listened carefully. There was no sign that it had been electrified, but he wasn't going to touch it until he was sure.

Two of his soldiers loomed out of the darkness and bent low, cautiously approaching the fence. One of them looked at a hand-held instrument to make sure that it wasn't electrified and then nodded. The second took bolt cutters, fashioned on ship but invented on Earth two hundred years earlier, and snipped the fence away from the post. The first grabbed the fence and bent it back out of the way.

Without a word, the remainder of the company was up and moving, filtering through the gap that had been cut and then spreading out again. They moved carefully, quietly, using hand signals and pointing. No one said a word. They fanned out and disappeared into the darkness and around the corners of the building.

Ramey moved with four others. They ran across the open ground and found a door without a knob on it. One of the soldiers reached out and touched it and was thrown back by the sudden shock. It was strong enough to knock him down but not enough to kill him.

"Simulated dead," said Ramey. He nodded at the next soldier. It was no longer necessary to remain completely quiet. He was sure the door was alarmed.

The man pulled a mass of pliable material from a pouch, formed it into a ball and threw it at the door. It hit with a wet smack and then detonated. The door blew in suddenly, smoke obscuring the entrance.

"Go!" yelled Ramey, his voice louder than he had intended it to be.

One woman ran into the door and was caught in a crossfire. She staggered back out, her harness buzzing and flashing. She should have fallen where she had been hit, but she wanted to warn the others.

"Automatic?" asked a voice.

Ramey didn't know. And he didn't know how to get into the building. He crouched away from it and tried to think of something, figuring that he still had a few moments.

A siren began to wail. First a low, nearly inaudible sound but it rose until it was screaming like a banshee searching for all who would die that night.

"Sir?" said one of the men.

"Grenades," said Ramey. "Five grenades. On my command."

Ramey slipped forward and knelt near the side of the door. He glanced at the others and counted. "One. Two. Three!" He tossed the grenade into the building and then dived to the left, using the wall of the building for cover.

The grenades detonated and Ramey was on his feet. Now he was aware of the dust in the air. He could taste the acrid smoke and found it hard to breathe.

Around him, others were attacking the structures. There were more sirens wailing, more grenades detonating, and now there was some shooting. Laser beams flashed in the dark, pencil-thin ruby-colored lights that cut through the night.

"Go!" yelled Ramey. He dived through the door and rolled to the right.

He raised his weapon but found nothing more than the smoking remains of the defensive weapons there. They had been smashed by the grenade attack.

But there was another door, this one looking as if it had been made of thick metal. He glanced at his watch. The attack had been under way for six minutes, and he needed to accomplish his mission in another seven.

He ran across the debris-littered floor and reached out but didn't touch the door. "Gibson. Get up here."

Gibson reported and saluted. "Yes, sir."

Ramey didn't say anything about the salute. He'd mention that during the critique later. Instead he said, "Check the door."

"Yes, sir."

She moved forward but didn't touch anything. She studied the side, searching for trip wires. She tried to find a switch or knob but found nothing.

"Hurry it up." Ramey was aware that time was running out. Losing the company wasn't the only way to fail the exercise. Hell, everyone could survive, but if the mission wasn't accomplished, then it was the same as a massacre.

Gibson set her weapon on the floor and turned slightly, grabbing at something in one of the pouches she wore. Just as she did, the door burst open and three men rushed out. One struck her on the side, knocking her down. He fired at her and set off her harness.

"Kill them," yelled Ramey as he fired.

The tiny room erupted into a firefight. Laser beams flashed and flared brightly. The harnesses buzzed with the simulated deaths of the soldiers. There was a shout, more of a primal scream, as one of the soldiers jumped at two of the enemy. They were knocked from their feet. Ramey leaped forward, the barrel of his laser against the chest of one of them. He fired, "killing" the man.

As he turned, he saw the other two go down, but he was alone now. The tiny force he'd brought into the building was simulated-dead around him.

Time was slipping away. He had to disable the defensive position before the main fleet entered the atmosphere to drop the division. He had to hurry.

Now he ran through the door and found a maze there. Doors and corridors that led right and left and up and down. He stood there for a moment and knew that he had failed. There was no way he could do anything to disable the battery.

A noise to his right caught his attention and he whirled in time. He killed the single man running at him. He probably couldn't disable the whole battery, but he could do something to it. And the rest of the company might be having better luck.

Figuring that the power source would be buried under as much protection as possible, he ran down the corridor that led into the bowels of the building. It was a narrow tiled corridor brightly lighted. There were no doors off either the right or left side. There were no sounds coming from it.

He reached the bottom and found another door. He stopped short of it. Time was fading away. The door looked as solid as rock. There were no way for him to get through it. He turned his laser on it and opened fire. It did no good.

Ramey turned and looked back up the corridor. He could

still hear the wailing of the siren but nothing else. No sounds of fighting.

Knowing that he'd failed, he ran back up the corridor. He stopped at the intersection and wondered where the rest of the company was. Maybe they'd had some luck. Maybe they'd damaged the facility. It was the only thing he could hope for.

He ran through the room where the firefight had taken place, looking at the simulated-dead. In a real fight, he would have stopped to see if there was anything he could do for them. Now, all he wanted to do was get out.

As he left the building, the overhead lights all came on. A voice boomed through the speakers. "The exercise has ended. The exercise has ended."

Ramey sat down then. Sweat beaded and dripped. He wiped at it and felt the hammering in his chest. He knew that he had failed.

Crowley approached and then stood, looking down at him. "You look like hell."

"Thanks. How'd it go?"

"We got caught in a crossfire. I got killed right away. Two of the people got inside, but they couldn't get through to the interior. They had to get out."

"That's what happened to me. Didn't accomplish much. You get any feel for the casualties?"

"No, sir. Just that it was bad."

Ramey saw a party approaching in the distance. He stood up and brushed at the seat of his pants. "Well, here it comes." He nodded at the newcomers.

"It was only an exercise," said Crowley.

"Yeah, I keep telling myself that. Well, let's go see what they have to say."

Together the two of them walked to the fence and then through it. Ramey didn't know if he should salute Jefferson or not. They were in a simulated combat environment even though the journalist, Garvey, was with the general. He decided to forget about saluting.

"General."

Jefferson grinned at him. "Not very good, Captain."

"We got inside," he said.

"And that was all that you did," said Torrence. "You did nothing to disrupt the ability of the facility to interdict our landing."

"If we'd had longer, we might have taken it out," said Ramey.

Jefferson shrugged. "But at what cost? Preliminary figures show over sixty percent casualties in your company. It might be that your force would have been eliminated without doing any real damage."

"Yes, General."

Torrence asked, "What was the problem?"

"Too many doors. We weren't expecting the set up on the inside." He turned and looked back at the building. He could see some of his soldiers coming out.

"Should have blown them," said Jefferson.

"Yes, sir. Didn't have the equipment to do it. Besides, there were so many of them I don't think we could have blown them all. That and try to maintain the sneak-and-peak end of the operation."

"Once the sirens went off, the enemy knew you were there and stealth made no difference. You should have used the grenade launchers to take out the doors. And you should have cleared each room with grenades. Never use a soldier when an explosive will do. We weren't trying to capture the facility. We were trying to destroy it."

"Then why not bomb it?"

Jefferson laughed. "A very good question. The difference is that there were defensive facilities that would be attacked from space, but from more than a hundred thousand feet, we can't be sure that a facility is destroyed. The only way to be sure is to send in troops. Besides, if we can eliminate them with ground forces, then the air assault might be able to get down without alerting the enemy to our presence. Besides, there are some very good reasons for a combat assault."

"Yes, General."

Garvey chimed in for the first time. "What would those good reasons be?"

Jefferson looked at Torrence and ignored the question that

Garvey had asked. "Anything that you want to say here, Colonel Torrence?"

"Just that I wish things could have progressed without the number of casualties. I don't want to see something like that in the real combat environment."

"Yes, ma'am."

Jefferson looked at his watch. "I think it's time to get out of here. Get your people together and head back out. Take the next twelve hours off."

"Yes, sir."

Torrence said, "Officer's call at noon tomorrow. We'll get the final assignments."

"That mean . . ."

Jefferson cut him off, thinking of the journalist standing behind him, and then realized that it didn't make any difference. There were no enemy spies on the ship to learn that the fleet was approaching the jump-off point. Ship scuttlebutt would give everyone the information inside an hour or two anyway. And Garvey wouldn't be able to file his story without Jefferson's approval for the use of the radio.

"That means," said Jefferson, "that we're about to go back to war."

8

JEFFERSON STOOD AT the head of the conference table and looked at the assembled officers. They were his three regimental commanders, the battalion commanders, and selected officers who would be handling special assignments during the drops. They had gone over the information several times, there had been exercises designed to familiarize the troops with the assignments, and there had been briefings to cover the new intelligence as the scouts brought it in, or as it was developed in debriefing the freed prisoners.

The attitude in the briefing room had changed. In the beginning, there had been jokes. There had been byplay among the officers, each extolling the virtues of his or her regiment or battalion. Now that was gone. The officers were sitting quietly, waiting for the general to give them the final, and in a few cases, the fatal word.

Jefferson glanced around the table, noticing the grim faces, the thin lips, and the black circles around the eyes. He noticed that the officers had the look of men and women who were about to receive a sentence from the judge which they all knew was going to be bad.

"First," he said, "let me say that initial landings will begin about twelve hours from now." He stared at Torrence. "Your regiment will lead it off."

"Yes, sir." There was no enthusiasm in her voice.

The holo of the enemy's industrial complex came up again. By now everyone was as familiar with it as they were with their home cities. They'd seen it dozens of times. Computer projections had rotated it, shown it from ground level, and had provided segmented portions of it so that officers leading raids would know exactly where to attack.

Jefferson stepped back and said, "Synchronized landings will begin before dawn. Raiders will have forty minutes to accomplish the destruction of the targets and then the main landing will begin. . . ."

"What about aerial bombardment?"

"Problem with that," said Jefferson, "is that it would tip our hand too early and we'd still have to land. If the raiders can do their jobs, casualties will be light and the fleet won't have to worry about getting in close." Jefferson glanced at his regimental commanders but said nothing about the prisoners. That was a secret the division commander wanted to keep. If the prisoners were found and freed, then public announcements would be made. If not, no one would ever know that the attempt had failed.

"And then?" asked one of the officers.

Jefferson knew what was being asked. He nodded and said, "If we run into trouble, we'll use the fleet to cover us. If all we were worried about was destroying the enemy, we could stand back and use nuclear weapons, turning the surface of the planet into a glowing, radioactive mess. We want to be able to use the resources here if we're going to the trouble of buying them with our blood." He was surprised that no one questioned that logic. They accepted it.

Jefferson stopped and turned. "Once the raiders have eliminated the defensive weapons, the remainder of the brigade will drop here, here and here and sweep into the city, securing it as quickly as possible. We will then hold until we're relieved. That shouldn't be more than seventy-two hours for all our units."

"Enemy space capability?"

"That'll be handled by the battle cruisers with us, and the division fleet as necessary. They'll attack anything moving in space that doesn't belong to us. We'll sweep their ships from space and destroy their capability to make war."

Jefferson stopped talking and moved away from the holo. "Each raider unit will secure his or her objective, and then hold in place until the remainder of the brigade is down to support them."

"What about counterattacks?"

"If the enemy should mount a counterattack, your first option is to repel it. Should that fail or should you be confronted with an overwhelming enemy force, then surrender the objective and get out as quickly as possible. The enemy, once they have retaken a position, will find that position worthless to them. You should have destroyed all equipment and supplies housed there."

"Yes, sir."

Jefferson glanced at the rest of the officers. "Anything else?"

"If we fail to take an objective?"

"I would hope that we wouldn't have to deal with that, but if we do, the first option is to call for reinforcements from the closest unit to you. If it requires a larger force, then we'll have people here who can drop. If all else fails, we can attempt to take it out from space. With enough of the defenses down, it shouldn't endanger the fleet."

"Yeah," said a voice. "I would sure be unhappy if the fleet was exposed."

Jefferson didn't try to identify the speaker. Instead he said, "If the fleet is crippled or destroyed, just how do you plan to get off the planet's surface?"

There was no answer to that.

Jefferson then reached down, touched the keyboard that darkened the holo display. The enemy's city vanished suddenly. There should have been a quiet pop as it did, but there was no sound.

Jefferson stepped to his chair, pulled it out and sat down. He looked at the assembled officers for a moment and then lowered his eyes. He knew that some of them would be dead in a few hours. Others would be badly hurt and the orders were his to give. He'd tell them to go and they'd do it. But before they did, he knew that he owed them an explanation.

"There is another reason that we don't just drop bombs and use the lasers and beams. We could, conceivably, destroy the enemy from space. But what would we gain from it? The ruins of a city and a technology provide us with nothing new. Nothing from which we can learn. But if we leave as much of the city intact as we can, there are opportunities to expand human knowledge in great leaps."

He looked up at them. "Think of what might have happened to human history if the Romans hadn't used the library of Alexandria to fire the baths and warm the water. What did the Mayans know that we lost when the Spanish burned their books? How many times did we have to learn the answers over and over because those with the knowledge were killed and their writings destroyed?"

"So we're going in to . . ." started Torrence.

"We're going in so that we can gain that knowledge. The intelligence officers think, and the general staff agrees, that these beings know more about space travel that we do. They have explored a larger part of the galaxy than we have. They have knowledge that we can use."

"So we're going to have to land on the surface of a hostile planet and trade lives for knowledge," said someone.

"Yeah," said Jefferson. "That's about it. In the long run . . . Oh hell." He fell silent for a moment. "Soldiers have often been used to advance civilization, to force religious views on others, to search for the Holy Grail."

"That's not the point," said an officer.

"Of course it is," said Jefferson. "We're the last resort. When everything else fails, send in the military. Military action is the last refuge of diplomatic policy. I'm sorry, but I find myself having to defend a position that I don't believe in myself. I agree with you. We should just bomb the fuckers back to the Stone Age, if they had one. But the decisions are not made by me or you."

"Made by men who never had to fight."

"There's nothing that I can do about it. Or that you can. I suppose, if anyone wants to surrender his or her command, I can find a replacement."

Torrence shook her head. "No, sir. We'll all stay."

"Okay," said Jefferson. "Colonel Torrence, you'll need to get your regiment to the drop bay. Have you made the specific assignments?"

"Yes, sir."

Jefferson nodded. "Then if there are no specific questions, I suggest that we get back to work."

As one, the men and women in the briefing room came to their feet.

Carson always told everyone that he liked being a scout because he didn't have to put up with the bullshit of the fleet, that he set everything himself, and that he could entertain himself on the long flights. But the truth was that he was often scared, and the words of the young technician on the ship haunted him. If something did go wrong, there was no one around to fix it but himself, and he wasn't convinced that he could fix *anything*, as he'd claimed.

And now, to make it worse, he was heading back toward the enemy's home planet to set up for the coming invasion. He had entered the enemy system with everything turned off that would emit a detectable signal except the life-support and lighting systems. Each used electrical power which generated an electrical field but the level was so low that it was easily masked by natural sources of energy. Carson didn't bother with the engines. They were shut down as he drifted, falling in toward Zeta Reticuli.

Using the charts he'd carried with him, he spotted the enemy's home planet, turned his ship and let the gravitational pull of the planets and the star drag him toward his target. He didn't use the viewplate but instead opened the cockpit screen so he could see out the transparent bubble on the top of his ship.

He was looking into the galactic center, though it was still thousands of light years away. On Earth, on a dark night, or from the moon, the Milky Way was an inspiring sight, but here in space, closer to it, it was unbelievable. A spill of stars so close together that they formed a glowing, pulsating band of bright light. Carson found himself staring at the Milky Way, unable to look away from it.

He sat for several minutes, his mind blank, the fear gone. The sight in front of him was too magnificent to ignore. And then, slowly, he let his eyes drift away, down to the bright points of light that marked the double star of Zeti Reticuli.

"Okay," he said outloud. "Let's get the ship turned."

He studied the stars and planets around him, spotted the dull blue marble that looked like the twin of Earth from so far out, and touched the controls of his ship. There was a puff of gas and the angle of the craft changed slightly.

"That'll do it," he said.

Instead of closing the screen, he fell back into the seat and stared up into space. He knew there was work to be done but he just couldn't get around to it. There was still plenty of time.

Ramey felt the excitement surge through him when the order finally came down. No more training exercises. No more practice runs. Now it was time to form the company and prepare for the drop. It was time to get the show on the road.

Ramey felt a sudden rush of adrenaline. He wanted to run or shout. He wanted to hurry, but couldn't. He had to remain calm and had to be seen as calm by the troops.

He found Crowley and said, "We need to get the troops and their gear down to the drop bay."

"Yes, sir."

He stood for a moment, grinning like a schoolboy. "This is it."

Crowley looked at him and he shrugged. Then, without a word, both of them started to run. Not because the mission demanded it, but because they had to. The energy was burning through them and there was no sign that release would come soon.

CHAIN OF COMMAND

They reached the company area and stood in front of the hatch as it irised open. Ramey leaped through and saw that chaos had erupted. The men and women of the first platoon were scrambling to get ready. They were yanking at their gear, piling it in the center of the room. They were pushing and shoving, rushing to get everything stacked.

The platoon sergeant wasn't helping. She was crouched near her cube, pulling out the knifes and weapons she'd stored in there. She was tossing aside videos, manuals, her blanket and anything else that wouldn't save her life in combat.

"Sergeant," yelled Ramey.

She glanced back over her shoulder, saw the captain and leaped to her feet. "Platoon! A-ten-SHUN!"

There was a momentary lull as the men and women slowed, wondering what had happened, and then they began falling in, dropping everything they held. One by one, they came to a position of attention.

Ramey nodded. "As you were." He watched as the soldiers bent back to work.

"Seems to be going okay in here," said Crowley.

"Yeah. You ready to go?"

"Gear is packed and waiting in my cabin. Just have to check the weapons and I'm ready."

Ramey nodded. "Me too."

Cooper wasn't happy when the word came down. He'd hoped that the battle would be avoided somehow. He didn't know how, short of an enemy surrender which didn't seem likely, but he hoped it could be. Now, standing in the center of the platoon bay, watching as his squad worked to get ready, Cooper felt as if he was about to die.

"Come on, Bill," said the squad leader. "We've got to move it."

"Yeah," answered Cooper, but he couldn't move. His arms and legs had turned to lead. He was suddenly lightheaded and felt like he was going to be sick to his stomach. He didn't want to move. Didn't want to think.

Someone bumped into him, pushing him to the side. The man looked up and said, "Sorry," and then rushed off.

But that was enough to get him moving. He crouched by his cube and reached inside. He touched the holo cube showing his family and his girl, and then pushed it aside wondering if he'd ever see them again.

He pulled his weapon free and stood, looking back at the rest of the people in his platoon, watching them work. They were excited, talking in bursts of energy. No one was walking. They were running. Nervous energy seemed to crackle in the air around them.

"Sarge," he said as she rushed by him again. He reached out to grab her sleeve and missed. But she stopped anyway.

"What?"

"This isn't just another exercise is it?" he asked. "Not just a drill?"

"This is the real thing." She glanced at him and then said, "Where's your vest?"

"In my cube."

"Get it. You're going to need it. And I want everyone ready to move out in ten minutes. Formed, with full equipment and weapons. I don't want to have to wait for someone to get ready. Ten minutes."

"Sure, Sarge."

Cooper turned again and saw that a couple of the people were standing around, talking in low tones. They wore their jump gear, backpacks and held their weapons. Each was dressed in a camouflaged combat uniform made from a fine wire mesh that could absorb the energy of a laser or particle beam and dissipate it. The uniform had gloves that covered most of the hand and a hood that covered the head and hid most of the face. They were ready to go.

Cooper felt the sweat drench him. Suddenly, it was as if he'd stepped into a shower wearing his uniform. Sweat dripped down his face and soaked his shirt. His breathing was ragged, sounding as if he'd just run ten miles.

The squad leader appeared. "You okay?"

"Yeah," said Cooper, nodding. "Just a little excited."

"Let's get with it," she said. "Five minutes."

"What happens in five minutes?"

"We move out to the drop bay. In formation. Ready to deploy to the planet's surface."

"Great," said Cooper.

He didn't mean it.

9

THE DROP BAY was alive with people. Technicians were running from one end of it to the other. Soldiers stood in formation, waiting to be loaded into the pods that stood in clusters of various sizes in the center of the bay. There was shouting and screaming and the ringing of a bell that no one seemed inclined to shut off.

Torrence stood with her back to a bulkhead and wondered if they'd ever get organized. She wanted to take a hand in it, but knew that the technicians didn't need guidance from her. Each was highly trained and responsible.

And the battalion, company and platoon commanders didn't need her help. They'd get their soldiers into the drop bays and into the pods without her adding to the confusion. For the first time, she understood how Jefferson must feel. There was no need for her to do anything except accept the blame if something went wrong.

A sergeant ran up, hesitated and then saluted, "Captain Davies says that all is ready, ma'am."

"Thank you, Sergeant."

Jefferson appeared at her side suddenly. "Looks like you'll be ready on time."

"If you say so." She stared at him, waiting.

"Just came down to wish you luck on your first combat drop."

"It's not my first."

"I meant you're first as the regimental commander. Mind if I give you a little advice?"

"No, General."

"Let the people under you do their jobs. Everyone is well trained, competent and intelligent. Listen to what they say, and let them do their jobs."

"I planned on that," she said.

Jefferson turned to watch the activity. "You know, it always looks like a fire drill where no one knows what he's supposed to be doing. People running in all directions."

"But it gets done," Torrence said.

"And done right," said Jefferson. He glanced at her and asked, "Are you okay?"

"I'm fine. Little nervous before the drop, but what do you expect?"

"You to be nervous." Jefferson lowered his voice. "For your ears only. There is a contingency plan in case the landing goes badly. Estimates are that we can get ninety percent of the attacking force off the planet in under an hour if it becomes necessary."

"What about the other ten percent?" she asked.

"They'll be the bodies we leave behind," said Jefferson. He waited a moment and then added, "I don't like sounding cold blooded, but if we have to evacuate, more than ten percent of the force will be dead anyway."

"Yes, sir."

"The main objective is still the citadel in the center of the city complex. That should be where the prisoners are being held. Get them out and back to the pickup zone as quickly as you can."

"That was my plan," said Torrence. She grinned briefly. "Once we've gotten them clear, then the bombers can come in if we need them."

Jefferson glanced around to make sure they were still alone. "If it gets bad, forget them. Pull back and we'll let the fleet take care of the problem. It would be nice to free them, but the safety of your regiment is of primary importance."

"I understand."

"Do not sacrifice the regiment to either take the citadel or to rescue the prisoners."

"Yes, sir."

Jefferson noticed that her answers were getting shorter and becoming perfunctory. "Vicki," he said, "you don't have to drop. It is acceptable for the regimental commander to remain here and coordinate using all the facilities of the ship."

"Would you remain behind?"

"No."

"I won't either. If the regiment drops, I drop with it. And if the regiment dies, I die with it."

There was a sudden, icy silence and then she blurted, "I didn't mean that the way it sounded."

"I know. We both should have died when the Tenth was lost." He was silent and then said, "Don't let it happen again. The Tenth only has so many lives."

"I'll protect it," she said.

A sailor approached and asked, "Will you be using the command pod?"

"Yes."

"We have it ready for you then, ma'am."

"I'll be there in a minute."

"Yes, ma'am. Thank you, ma'am." The sailor whirled and rushed off.

"Looks like I've got to go," she said.

"Good luck, Vicki." Jefferson hesitated and then grinned broadly. "Don't forget that I love you."

"Yes, General. I'll remember."

She then hurried off, following the path taken by the sailor. She approached the command ring, five pods hooked together and set up for the command staff. Members of her staff would be dropping in them. The rest of the soldiers would drop in platoon sized rings, one pod for each soldier, hooked together in rings of forty pods.

A sailor opened the front of the pod and Torrence turned and backed into the warm gel that surrounded her body, seeming to

CHAIN OF COMMAND

hug her. The sailor waited until she nodded and then he closed the lid carefully. If it hadn't been for the dull blue glow and the heads-up display, it would have been like being sealed into a coffin.

She activated the radio. "Apache Six to control."

"Control. Go."

"Latest intell?"

"Transmitting now."

The heads-up in front of her flashed and information began to parade across it. She scanned it quickly, learning that there was a thick cloud cover of the target area, and it looked as if there was some kind of precipitation falling. That would cover the descent and make it harder on the enemy to spot them. Nothing to worry about.

She then switched channels and saw that all units that were going to land with the first wave had reported in and were ready for the drop. Nothing to do but sit back and let the ship's pilots do their jobs. Let them drop the pods when they were ready.

Inside the pod, she could feel nothing. If it hadn't been for the information scrolling on the heads-up, she knew that she would have panicked. She was sealed in a pod that didn't allow her to move much. The gel flowed and ebbed around her body, letting her flex her muscles, but it was always there, a warm, pulsating mass.

The worst part of being sealed in the pod was freefall. She had been told repeatedly that she couldn't feel freefall, but that didn't matter. She believed she could. The pod compensated for everything from the air pressure changes to the freezing cold of space and the heating as they fell through the atmosphere, and still Torrence believed she could feel those changes. The slightest malfunction and she would be quick frozen, or fried, or splattered over half a mile of enemy terrain.

"Approaching drop point," said one of the controllers. "Two minutes to drop."

Torrence took in a deep breath and was scared. Before there had been Jefferson to rely on. Jefferson, as the commander, had to make the decisions. She could listen and object, but in the end, he was there to take the responsibility.

Now there was no one but her. She had to make the decisions. There was no one else to take the blame. There was no one but her. It was her job.

"One minute. Please signal all ready."

Torrence reached out and touched a button. It would light a bulb on a panel in the control room. That was a new feature, one that she was sure had been installed to make the troops happy. It gave them the feeling that they had the option to abort the drop if they detected anything wrong in their pod. Of course, it was unlikely that they would be able to spot anything wrong once they had been sealed inside.

"We have a clean board."

"Tenth is ready," she said unnecessarily.

"Roger, Apache Six."

"You have thirty seconds."

Torrence felt her stomach grow cold. This was going to be a nasty one. They weren't dropping into some primitive world where the enemy might be armed only with crossbows or single-shot rifles. They were dropping onto an industrialized world where the beings had space travel. It was not going to be easy.

"Fifteen seconds."

Torrence tensed, as if she had to physically push herself into space. She knew the routine now. The ship dropping into the outer reaches of the planetary atmosphere, the opening of the drop floor and the release of the pods. The ship would be in the atmosphere for ten, maybe fifteen seconds. Once the pods were away, it would be climbing out, heading into space, out of range of lasers and beams and missiles.

There was no word from the control room and there was no real sensation. Torrence was suddenly aware of the numbers on the heads-up unreeling as they were falling toward the ground. As she realized that, she felt suddenly sick to her stomach. They'd be on the ground in minutes.

She scanned the heads-up, learning that all pods had deployed and so far there were no malfunctions. Everything was in the green.

And there was no indication that they had been spotted by the enemy. No sensor scans, no radar echoes. No electronic sweeps. Now she wouldn't broadcast except in an extreme emergency. Nothing to tell the enemy they were coming.

She heard the chute deploy and felt a slight tug, more of a bounce as the chutes inflated. The numbers were no longer a blur as the descent slowed thanks to the chute. She took a deep breath and tried not to think about a chute failure.

Seconds later the chute released the pod and the rockets fired, slowing her even more. She took another deep breath. Now the air tasted metallic, recycled, just like the atmosphere on the ship.

The jets kept firing, slowing her. There was a gentle bump and she was down on the planet's surface. The pod's lid popped open, and Torrence found that she was tilted at an angle, facing down, looking at the ground. She pushed herself free and stepped into the night of the enemy's planet. She slipped and fell to her back, looking up at a gentle glow. All she could see was the snow falling rapidly.

She used her short-com. "Commanders, report down."

She listened as they reported in, one by one, in order. Everyone had gotten out of the ship and everyone had reached the planet's surface.

She rolled over and pushed herself up, staring into the blinding white of the blowing snow. She turned and noticed that the pods were streaming through their camouflage colors, trying to match the surroundings, but the paint patterns had not been designed with a blizzard in mind.

Using the image enhancer of her helmet, she tried to see the city but the snow was too thick. All she got was white. It was the same as being snow blind.

Ramey appeared and stood next to her. He kept his voice low. "We're set to go."

"Any problems?"

"No, ma'am. Everyone made it."

Torrence tried to see something, anything. The wind was picking up now and beginning to howl. Everything around them was white. The pods stood out like a mess a dog had made. The camouflage of the uniforms had been designed with the city in mind. There were bands of black in it that would do them no good in the arctic-type environment.

"Someone sure blew it," said Ramey.

Torrence ignored that and tried to get her bearings. The heads-up indicated the city off to the right. She turned but could see nothing there, other than the snow.

"No one even thought of snow," she said. She glanced at Ramey. "You had better get moving. We don't have that much time."

"I doubt the enemy knows we're down," he said.

"Go."

Ramey ran off, disappearing into the swirling white mass. He just seemed to fade away. There was a silence around her. A deadening of the noise she expected as the soldiers formed to move out. The snow blanketed it, dampening out the sound.

Two soldiers loomed out of the white. They stopped and seemed to be waiting. She knew that they were the bodyguard assigned to her.

Torrence checked the heads-up but there was nothing from the other units showing. No one would contact her unless something had gone terribly wrong.

She moved back toward the pods. The intelligence officer was crouched near one, down out of the wind. Snow was piling up around him.

Leaning close, she said, "What the hell happened?"

"What do you mean?"

"I mean that none of you predicted a snowstorm. I was told there was some precipitation. Not that there would be a fucking blizzard."

"It's no problem," said the intell officer.

"Oh, no," snapped Torrence. "Everything is fine. Just tell me where in the hell the enemy city is."

The man stood, brushed the snow from his face and then pointed. "Over there."

"I sure as hell hope you're right." She turned but could see nothing. She pushed her way through the snow, finding that it was drifting. In one place it came up to her knees and in another was almost to her waist. "Shit!"

She found Ramey and shook her head. "Let's get going here."

"Yes, ma'am. Just trying to consolidate the company."

"I want you moving now."

"Yes, ma'am." He turned and shouted. "First platoon, you move out now."

She was going to stop the shouting and then realized that it probably didn't matter. There would be no enemy soldiers around to hear and the snow would keep the noise from traveling.

She watched as a dozen soldiers ran by her. They disappeared into the blizzard. She caught up with Ramey and asked, "Where's the second platoon?"

"Over there. Lieutenant Crowley is with them. She'll be leading their raid."

"And third?"

"To the far right. Lieutenant Malone is leading them."

"I'll be with Malone."

"Yes, ma'am. We're on our way now."

"Remember. You've got forty-five minutes to knock out the defensive guns."

"I understand."

As Ramey made his way off into the snow, Torrence hurried toward the third platoon. The question that kept swirling in her mind was, "Why couldn't they have told me it was snow?"

10

JEFFERSON STAYED IN the control room until the initial drop had been made. He sat buckled into one of the control chairs, facing a screen that showed him little other than the swirling patterns of clouds over the planet's surface and the pinpoints of light that had been the pods before they slipped under the slate-gray clouds.

On the instruments, he watched as the pods, cloaked in charcoal fell into the night. He knew the moment the chutes deployed, and he knew when the rockets fired. He knew the instant they touched the ground, but that's all he knew. Radio blackout kept the soldiers from reporting because any signal strong enough to be detected by the fleet could be detected by the enemy. Silence, swiftness and stealth were the allies of the soldiers on the ground.

Because there was nothing else for him to do, Jefferson stood up. He took a final look at the drop bay where the technicians and sailors were struggling to get the next wave ready.

"I'll be on the bridge," he said.

"Yes, General," acknowledged one of the controllers without looking up from his console.

CHAIN OF COMMAND

Jefferson knew that they didn't care where he was, as long as it wasn't in the control booth with them. He stepped to the hatch, let it iris open and moved out into the corridor.

It too was filled with activity. The soldiers of the battalion that would drop next filled it, waiting for access to the drop bay. They were a quiet, somber bunch, with NCOs moving along the lines, checking names, checking equipment and inspecting weapons. Make-work to keep everyone busy so they didn't have time to think about climbing into a coffin-sized pod to be dropped into the hostile environment of the enemy's home planet.

Jefferson walked along it slowly, heading for the mid-lift that would take him to the bridge. He wanted to run, but was afraid his excitement would spread to the soldiers, causing trouble.

He reached the mid-lift, entered it and rode it to the level of the bridge. He exited and walked down the corridor. Here, it looked as if the ship was deserted. No one in the corridors. They were all at their stations, working.

Jefferson entered the bridge, another hub of activity. There were sailors everywhere, some of them standing two and three deep behind positions, watching everything that was going on in front of them. They were going to make sure that they covered each position so that the troops on the ground had everything they needed.

No one noticed Jefferson as he entered. He moved down the two steps so that he stood behind the captain's chair, staring up at the flatscreens displaying information.

"How goes it, Captain?" he asked.

The woman turned and looked back at Jefferson. "It goes fine," she said. She nodded at the center screen. "Cloud cover is causing us trouble."

"What's it like on the ground?"

"Right now, we can't tell anything. First wave is down and there doesn't seem to be any resistance. We've got no reports from the ground and that's the good news."

"Can we punch through the clouds to get a look?"

"Yes, General, but that'll produce radiation they'll be able to read."

"Right." Jefferson took a step forward, toward the main screen where the swirling mass of the planet's cloud cover was shown.

"You hear anything," said Jefferson, "I want to know immediately."

"Goes without saying."

Carson touched his controls to nudge his ship forward slightly. He was in a parking orbit over two hundred miles above the planet's surface. He was keeping a visual watch on the planet, and he was prepared to activate a beacon if the incoming vessels needed additional guidance.

He'd been in the perfect position to watch as the first of the soldiers had been dropped to the planet's surface, not that it was much of a show. The ship, painted dull black, had been hard to see against the darkness of space. Everything had been well masked so that it was hidden from the enemy's sensors, radars and detectors.

There had been a momentary flash of light as the drop bay doors had opened. There had been a rush of residual air that might have been seen from the ground if the enemy had been looking with the proper equipment.

The deployment pods, also jet black, had fallen free of the ship as it turned, using the planet's gravity to throw itself back into space. The pods had been impossible to see visually once they were clear of the ship. Carson had used his flatscreen and image enhancer. Then he could make out the rings of pods, but just barely. There was no way to find them, unless the enemy had a motion-detection system that could screen out all the debris circling their planet.

The pods had fallen, heating slightly as they entered the planet's atmosphere. That had been detectable, but again, the radiation was so slight that the enemy would have to know where to look to find them and then it was an even bet they'd miss them.

Now, with the pods on the ground, Carson had nothing to do. Stay in orbit and watch as the rest of the invasion force and the fleet approached. He was a picket, whose job it was to watch for signs that the enemy had found them. He was to provide intelligence if he gathered any, and he was to guide the invasion ships if they needed it.

He reached out and touched a button on his flatscreen, changing the view. The cloud deck over the industrial complex was too thick to penetrate with convention methods. If he wanted to see what was happening on the ground, he'd need to use his instrumentation and that produced detectable radiation.

Shifting in his seat, he looked back over his shoulder to where the fleet was supposed to be. Without using a telescope, he could see nothing other than the ever-present star fields. He could see no sign of the fleet, and that was just the way it should be.

"Couple of hours," he said out loud, "and they'll all be here."

Without having to look at any of the flatscreens, Clemens knew that the fleet was strung out in formation around him. They had separated so that a single, well-placed missile couldn't get them all, but they could still protect one another if they were attacked.

He pushed himself out of the captain's chair and walked toward the flatscreens. It wasn't that he needed to see them better, he just felt the need to stand and move. He stood in front of the main screen and watched the dirty blue marble that was the enemy's home world.

"Message from Jefferson, Captain. He says that the first regiment is down, and there have been no reports of resistance."

"Thank you."

"Aye, sir."

Clemens turned and looked at the map showing the deployment of his fleet around him. They had formed two thin lines so that they looked like a giant plus sign flying through space. The theory was that one of the ships would be able to respond to a threat while the rest of the fleet redeployed.

The space around them was filled with tiny red specks. That marked the locations of the cap. Fighters sent out to the extreme ranges of the sensors so that the eyes and ears of the fleet would be able to see and hear farther. No one expected the fighters to attack an enemy fleet unless they could be regrouped for the attack. They were picket ships.

Clemens turned. "Time to next landing?"

"About ten hours. It'll be the rest of Jefferson's brigade. Landings of the rest of the division and other divisions will begin about a few hours after that."

Clemens took another good look at the screens. There was nothing for him to do. The sailors knew their jobs and the captains of the other ships had their orders. He had nothing to do but sit in his chair and watch as others worked.

He moved to the rear and then sat down. He studied the screens looking for something that he might have missed. A way to deploy the ships that would make the formation tighter, safer and deadlier for the enemy. But without knowing where the enemy was, of if an attack would come, there was nothing more to be done.

Turning, he asked, "We have any reports from the pickets?"

"No, Captain. Everything is quiet. The enemy doesn't know we're here."

"Give me a full three-sixty-degree scan on the center screen."

"Aye, Captain."

Clemens studied the screen as the cameras slowly revolved showing him everything around his ship. He caught glimpses of the other ships in the formation, of space debris orbiting, of meteors and dust, of moons and other planets. He caught sight of Jefferson's ships, maneuvering toward the enemy's planet for the next drop, and he saw his own ships, spread out in their defensive formation.

"Cut to a straight-ahead view."

"Aye, Captain."

Now there was little to see other than the enemy's home world. Clemens watched it, searching for a sign that the enemy was aware of the attack that was coming.

"Captain," said one of the sailors, "are we sure that we've got the right place?"

"Of course," snapped Clemens. "What an idiotic thing to say." But in his own mind, he was reviewing the intelligence that had dictated the decision. Everything they had gathered suggested that the enemy's home world was here.

But then Clemens knew what the people of Earth had done to protect their home. The battles had been fought ten or twelve light years from Earth. So far from the cradle of humanity that astronomers on Earth, if they could see the flashing lights of that battle, would be unable to detect if for another eleven years.

The people of Earth would throw everything into the battle to protect their home. There would be scout ships out and then a fleet, larger than anything deployed outside the solar system, to engage the enemy. Before he was allowed to land, there would be one massive space battle.

Trap? he wondered. Could the enemy be luring them into a trap so that they could be eliminated? Of course, there had been no sign that the enemy was setting a trap either.

"Where is their fleet?" Clemens asked quietly, but no one on the bridge responded.

"Captain, we've lost one of the pickets."

"On screen."

"Aye, sir."

The scene shifted abruptly. He could see that it was to the right of his position, near one of the gas giants on the outskirts of the enemy system. There was a flashing light where the picket should be.

"Full magnification?"

"Aye, sir."

There was nothing visible there. Just a magnificent planet that looked as if there was a faint ring system and a dozen moons around it. A golden planet with a huge green spot floating on the surface.

"Sensor probes?"

"Haven't initiated them, sir."

"Go ahead," said Clemens. "Enemy won't be looking for our radiation in that direction."

"Aye, sir."

"Report," said Clemens a moment later.

"Nothing on the sweep sir."

"Should you be able to detect the picket?"

"If he's still there, we should be able to find him, even if he's lost all systems."

Clemens asked, "Are all the other pickets still on their stations?"

"Aye, sir."

Clemens ran a hand through his short-cropped hair. He could feel the sweat begin to bead as his body temperature rose because he was now concentrating. This was what he was paid for. Now it was becoming critical. The picket could have crashed into the planet, he could have blown up, or he could have left his station for a variety of reasons. If his radios were out, if all his communications systems were gone, for whatever reason, he would not be able to report to the ship. At the moment, the disappearance was nothing to worry about. It was something to be concerned about and it was something to watch, but it was nothing more than a single ship disappearing.

"I want a complete sensor sweep of that entire area," said Clemens.

"Looking for, Captain?"

"The ship. Debris. An ionization trail. Anything that will tell us what happened to the picket."

"Aye, sir."

Clemens had been about to leave the bridge. He'd been thinking about a cup of coffee but now he knew he couldn't go get it. Not with a picket that had disappeared. He kept telling himself that it wasn't important, but somehow he just didn't believe it.

11

COOPER COULD SEE nothing around him. The snow was falling too hard, and the wind was whipping it around, filling the air with a white cloud that made it impossible to see more than a foot or two. There was a black shape to his right and he knew that had to be Cheryl Haggerson. She was the assistant gunner. Cooper had no idea where the machine-gunner was. He hoped that Haggerson could see him.

He was moving forward slowly, leaning into the wind, trying to find his target. It was supposed to be there somewhere, but the snow was hiding it as effectively as the best camouflage ever designed.

Using the short-com, he said, "Franz, I can't see a damn thing."

"Roger that. Wait one."

Cooper wanted to stop. He wanted to sit down but didn't. The one thing was that he wasn't very cold. His fingers were exposed, as were his eyes and a section of his forehead, but the rest of his body was covered by his uniform. It was as good as thermal underwear.

He shifted his weapon from his right hand to his left, making sure he didn't get a kink in the cable that connected his weapon to the power pack. Satisfied, he stuck the fingers of his right hand under his armpit, trying to warm them.

"Bill, I've lost Jason."

Cooper tried to ignore that for a moment. He didn't want to hear it. And then he slipped to the right to find Haggerson.

"Who's lost?" asked Franz.

Cooper didn't want to say a thing about that. He wanted to solve the problem, and then no one would have to know that Jason Baker was lost.

He found Haggerson standing with her back to him. She had a hand up over her eyes, staring into the swirling snow. It was already caked to her uniform, masking the dark colors.

"When'd you last see him?"

"Minute ago." She raised her voice although the wind wasn't making much noise.

"Franz, we need to halt for a moment," said Cooper.

"Roger. Take five."

To Haggerson, Cooper said, "We keep each other in sight. We look for his footprints."

"Snow'll cover it up."

Cooper knew that. But he hoped there would be a clue in the snow about Baker. "Just keep your eyes open."

"Yes, Corporal."

Cooper raised a hand and wiped the snow from his face. Ice was beginning to form on his hood. The snow was stinging his eyes, making it difficult to see.

Now he was breathing hard. The snow was knee deep around him, sometimes drifting as high as his waist. It was almost impossible to force his way through some of the drifts.

He scanned the ground, looking for signs of the missing man. He used the short-com. "Baker. Say location."

There was no response, except for Franz. "You have two minutes."

Cooper stopped moving and tried to see through the curtain of snow. He listened but heard nothing. He turned, but now Haggerson was missing too.

Then suddenly from Haggerson, he heard, "I've found him. I've found him."

Cooper turned and took two steps to the right. He spotted the

CHAIN OF COMMAND

dark shape of Haggerson crouched. He ran to her and saw that Baker was lying face down in the snow.

"Dead," she said. "Frozen." She pointed to a rip in the rear of the mesh of his uniform. "Don't know what happened to him here."

Cooper reached down and tried to slip a hand under the hood to search for a pulse. The skin was cold and unyielding. It was obvious that Baker was dead. There was no sign that he'd been shot, stabbed, beaten or attacked in any way. It looked as if his equipment had let him down. A flaw of some kind developed in the mesh, let in cold air, and that killed him.

"Get his gear," said Cooper.

"We're going to leave him?"

"For the moment there's nothing else that we can do," said Cooper.

"But . . ." she said and then fell silent. She knew as well as Cooper that the dead had to be left for the people in graves registration.

Cooper pushed the earpiece of his short-com deeper into his ear and then said, "Franz, we've one dead."

"Roger that. Rejoin us now."

"Roger." He glanced at Haggerson. "You are now the machine-gunner."

"Yes, Corporal."

Together they turned and headed back the way they had come, but Cooper couldn't see the rest of the platoon. He tried to spot the path they'd cut through the snow, but it was drifting closed already.

Using the short-com, he said, "Franz, we're having some trouble here."

"Roger. Look for the light."

Cooper knew that she had ignited a flare and pointed it at him, but he couldn't see it. The veil of drifting and blowing snow was too thick. He lifted a hand, trying to shield his eyes as he stumbled forward.

"Say location," asked Franz.

"I have no idea," said Cooper. "I do not have you in sight yet."

"We are falling behind schedule," Franz warned. "Let's speed it up."

"We're trying to find you," said Cooper. He thought the signal on the short-com was getting stronger. The range was so short that had he moved slightly away, signal strength would fall off.

"We're going to have to move out," said Franz.

Suddenly through the snow, he saw the red glow of the flare. "I've got you in sight."

"Roger that."

The flare faded then and Cooper was on the radio. "I've lost you." The glow reappeared and a moment later he saw Franz's shape through the snow.

He pushed forward and found his squad leader standing in front of him. She looked like a snowman, the snow clinging to her uniform and her weapon.

She whirled without a word and dropped the flare into the snow. It melted its way down and then was extinquished by the moisture.

Cooper fell in behind her. He kept her, Haggerson and two other squad members in sight. They no longer maintained much of an interval. They were trying to stick together, searching for the target.

Over the short-com, someone said, "We've come up against a fence."

"That's close enough," said Franz. She increased the pace, heading toward the fence.

Through the snow, Cooper could see a washed out amber glow. He saw Franz slip to one knee and raise her image enhancer to her eyes. The squad spread out in a loose circle.

Cooper moved closer to the squad leader. "That it?" he asked.

"Shit," said Franz, "I don't know. I can't see enough of it to tell. Could be."

"There's nothing else around here," said Cooper. "That's got to be it."

Cooper tried to remember the diagrams he'd seen. The computer-generated pictures of it flashed in his mind. But he

CHAIN OF COMMAND

couldn't see enough of the structure through the snow to be sure they were right.

"I think that's it," said Cooper. "I don't know."

Franz lowered her image enhancer and looked directly at him. He could only see her eyes because her eyebrows were now hidden by snow.

"Thompson, cut the fence," Franz ordered.

One of the soldiers moved forward and knelt near the fence. It didn't look like the chain-link fences they had practiced on in the ships. It was a wire mesh. Looking at the bottom of it, Cooper noticed that the ground was visible. No snow covering it.

"Hold it," yelled Cooper. He glanced at Franz. "Something's wrong here."

She nodded. "Blow it."

Thompson pulled the explosive from his pouch, rolled it into a tube and began to shove it under the bottom of the fence. It seemed to snag and then there was an audible click.

"Shit!"

The explosion ripped the fence apart. Bits of it shot through the air like shrapnel from a grenade. Thompson was thrown back. The front of his uniform blossomed bright red and his blood stained the snow.

"Scatter," said Franz.

Cooper hit the ground and rolled to the right. He kept his eyes on the dark shape in front of him. He was sure it was a building. He waited for an alarm to sound or flash, but nothing happened.

Franz was up on her feet, running for the hole in the fence. Over the short-com, she said, "Follow me."

Cooper jumped up and ran. He skirted the smoking crater created by the explosion. He glanced at Thompson and saw that one of his legs and both his arms were missing.

He caught up to Franz. He didn't tell her they had yet to engage the enemy and they'd already taken about twenty percent casualties. He was sure she was aware of it.

"What happened?" he asked.

"Current in the fence detonated the explosive. Tough luck."

"Yeah. Especially for Thompson."

"Find the door," she said.

Cooper ran forward through the knee-deep snow toward the dark shape. He reached it and realized that it was not a building but a pile of debris. Maybe it was garbage or maybe it was building supplies that had yet to be used. There was no door in it.

He ran around it and spotted another soft glow. He headed toward it. As he approached, the shape changed slightly and became a building. There was a door in the center of the wall. Snow was piled against it showing that no one had opened it since the storm had started.

He slowed down when he reached the wall. There was no sign of a window, an alarm or booby trap. He walked toward it and then crouched near it. He reached out but didn't touch it.

"We've got to blow it," said Haggerson.

Cooper shook his head but knew Haggerson was right.

"Anyone found a door?" asked Franz.

"Cooper here. I've got one. Looks like it's in the center of the wall."

"Wait one. I'll be there."

Cooper pointed at Haggerson. "Cover the approach. Facing the way we came."

"Right, Corporal."

Cooper turned back and inspected the door. There was nothing remarkable about it. It looked to be metal and there was no knob on it. The metal looked as if it was reinforced by steel bars. There didn't seem to be any way to open it.

Franz appeared out of the swirling snow. She stopped, studied the door for a moment and then said, "Blow it off its hinges."

Cooper couldn't see any hinges, but he didn't say anything about it. He pulled some explosive from his pouch, formed it into a ball, but then tossed it underhanded at the edge of the door where a knob would be if it had one.

As he tossed it, Cooper dived to the side, stretching out like a swimmer starting a race. He covered his head with his hands, dropping his rifle into the snow. When there was no explosion, he rolled to his side and grinned sheepishly at Franz who hadn't moved.

CHAIN OF COMMAND   89

"Check your weapon," she said.

Cooper used his hand to search the snow covering his rifle. Then he grabbed the cable that attached it to the powerpack on his belt and found it. He lifted it out of the snow, brushed it clean and grinned.

"It's fine."

"Let's blow the door," said Franz.

Cooper moved to it, looked at the explosive and then added a detonator and a timer. "Thirty seconds."

The squad scattered, spreading out into the snow, watching for signs that the enemy was coming up behind them. A moment later there was a quiet, hissing pop as the explosive blew a hole in the door. When they turned, the door still stood.

"Damn it," said Franz. "We've got to move. Let's go."

Cooper stepped to the door, leaned back and kicked once, his foot hitting the solid metal. There was a metallic clunk and then the door toppled in slowly. It hit the floor with a quiet, dull thud.

"There."

Franz waved a hand and pointed at the interior. Two soldiers rushed passed her, entered the building and then dived for cover.

Cooper had flattened himself against the wall, waiting for the burst of enemy fire from the inside. That never happened. As soon as the others were inside, Cooper followed them.

The interior was dark, but it was warm. The contrast to the blizzard outside was startling. Cooper felt the snow that clung to his uniform begin to melt.

"Go," yelled Franz.

Cooper pushed his way through the room to the wall opposite him. He could feel the warmth of the material. It felt like plastic, but he couldn't be sure.

"There a door?"

"Not that I can find."

"Christ," said Franz. "We've got to penetrate deeper."

"Here," yelled Haggerson. "I think I've found it."

"Open it," ordered Franz.

Light flared into the room. Noise assaulted them. Cooper pushed his way forward to the side of the door and glanced through. There was nothing on the other side of the door except an empty, lighted room.

"This doesn't look to be it," said Cooper.

"Come on," said Franz. "We've got to move."

As she tried to run by, Cooper grabbed her arm. He lowered his voice and said, "This doesn't seem to be the right place. You'd thing that a defensive complex would be guarded."

"You don't know what they'd do," said Franz. "Just search the damn building."

"Sure, Sarge," said Cooper. But he didn't know where to search. The room was empty.

"Got a door open over here," yelled someone.

Cooper turned and saw a corridor leading down into the bowels of the building.

"We've only got a few minutes left," said Franz.

Cooper ran forward, his weapon held in both hands. He stopped and looked down. Nothing to be seen anywhere. No evidence that the enemy was around.

"I don't think this is the right place," said Cooper.

"I don't care," snapped Franz. "We're going to destroy it. Get going."

Without a word, he started down, sure that they were wasting their time.

12

THE WEATHER WAS getting so bad that Torrence wondered if they shouldn't abandon the attack and evacuate everyone. They couldn't see their targets, communications were being disrupted, and she wasn't sure the next wave would be able to land. The snow was getting deeper, the wind was blowing harder and visibility was nearly gone.

She moved to the right, through the knee-deep snow and found Ramey standing with his image enhancer up against his eyes. "You see anything?"

"Nothing. I think we've got the glow from the city in that direction, but hell, it's impossible to see."

"We've got to get out of here," said Torrence. "You have to get your company moving."

"Yes, ma'am." Ramey lowered the image enhancer. "Just where do we go?"

"If the weather is this bad, the enemy won't be able to see us either. Let's get into the city and tear up a little real estate. Head in the general direction of the center of the city. That's our objective."

"Yes, ma'am."

"We've got to free the prisoners," said Torrence. "Sooner we do that, the sooner we can get the hell out of here."

"Yes, ma'am." Ramey turned away from her and tried to run along the line but the snow was too deep. He ran with the motion of a man stuck in molasses.

Torrence began walking toward the distant glow. That had to be the industrial complex. It was the only thing they could see through the swirling, blowing snow that was burying everything.

The soldiers of the company caught up with her and moved with her on line. But Torrence could only see a couple of the soldiers. They were little more than dark shapes barely visible in the storm.

Torrence found that it was nearly impossible to walk in the snow. It clung to the body and tugged at her legs. She struggled to move forward, trying to kick a path. Her head was down as she pushed her way forward.

Over the short-com, she heard, "I've lost sight of the column."

"Heading toward the glow. Drift toward it."

"Yes, sir."

Torrence took a step and fell to her waist. She struggled forward, grabbed at the snow as if to pull herself clear and worked her way up out of the snow.

"Found a fence," said a voice on the short-com. "Directly in front of us."

"Breach it," said Ramey on his short com.

"Yes, sir."

Torrence stopped and used her heads-up display. She could see an indication, infrared, that the city was in front of them. She turned and could see, using the infrared, the bodies of the closest soldiers. They were blue blobs of light struggling toward the city.

"Got a wall."

"Climb it," said Ramey on the short-com.

"Negative. Part of a building."

"Defensive structure?"

"I don't think so."

"Then work your way around to the side of it and keep moving."

"Yes, sir."

Torrence used her short-com. "Has anyone seen any sign of the locals?"

Ramey was first up. "Negative. Platoon leaders report in platoon order."

"One, negative."

"Two, negative."

"Three, negative."

Torrence said, "Let's stay alert."

They came to a concrete street. Across it there seemed to be a single building. Lights glowed in a couple of the windows and above a door.

"Let's hold it," said Ramey.

Torrence slid along the line until she reached Ramey. "We've got to move around it. We're not supposed to hold position. We're letting time slip away."

"Colonel," said Ramey, "let's suppose that the enemy spots us and tries to recall all their people. In this weather, how fast do you thing they could respond?"

"The point is that we're to take out the defensive positions and get to the prisoners before the second wave is dropped. The orders are explicit."

"We've got movement on the right."

"Deploy," said Ramey.

"Hold your fire until you identify the targets," said Torrence. In that weather, she didn't want one unit shooting up another.

She turned to face the incoming shapes. They didn't seem to look right on the heads-up, but the weather could be playing tricks on her. The heat signatures looked to be warmer than those of her own troops.

"Stand by," she said. And then suddenly she knew that they were being attacked. "Open fire. Open fire! We've got the enemy coming at us."

She whirled and knelt, lifting her laser rifle. In the mess of blowing snow, she saw a single, small shape. She fired at it, the laser beam stabbing out. But the snow got in the way and the beam bounced around the crystals, flashing.

Now there were others joining the one she had seen. More of her soldiers were firing, lighting the night with the brilliant flashes of red. It seemed as if the sky was beginning to bleed.

The enemy came closer, not firing in return. There was screaming from them. High-pitched wails that could have been pain, or anger, or surprise.

"Coming up on our right flank," yelled someone.

"Got one here."

"Careful with the lasers. Pick your targets."

Torrence lowered her weapon as the single shape she'd fired at disappeared, falling into the snow. She used the heads-up, spotted another two enemy but didn't fire. Her own people were too close.

Something seemed to rise up out of the snow at her feet. Torrence turned on it, but it was too close to shoot. She swung around, coming up with the butt of her rifle. She struck it solidly on the point of the chin, and it went down, disappearing into the light powder.

The fighting was now hand to hand with only an occasional burst from a laser. The beam would stab out and disappear into the violently blowing snow. Aiming was next to impossible. No one could tell where the beams were going.

Torrence took a step to the rear and used the heads-up display. The images of her soldiers were mixed with those of the enemy. There were brightly glowing lumps in the snow that marked the wounded of both sides. A few were fading rapidly as the body heat drained from them.

"Got them on the run," yelled a voice.

Torrence watched as the two sides separated suddenly, the enemy fleeing the way it had come. Torrence wasted no time. "After them! Kill them!"

She took a step forward and then slipped in the snow. She fell to one knee and then struggled to stand up. She ran forward, watching the enemy shapes in the heads-up. As she caught one of them, its glow seemed to overwhelm the equipment. She snapped it out of the way and saw the creature in front of her, caught next to a wall.

Before she should react, it turned and leaped for her, grabbing at her throat. Torrence fell back, but the fall was cushioned by the snow. She couldn't use the ground for leverage, the snow was too deep.

The beast fell on her and tried to rip the hood from her head.

Torrence lost her grip on her rifle. She balled her fist and struck the being on the side of the head. There wasn't a burst of pain like there would have been if she'd hit a human on the skull. The bone seemed soft.

But it was enough. The creature reached up and grabbed the side of its head with its long fingers. It slipped and as it did, Torrence rolled to her side. She got a hand under her and shoved, forcing herself to her feet. The creature fell into the snow. Torrence kicked once, like she was trying for a fifty yard field goal, felt her foot connect and heard the snapping of bone as the creature flipped to its back.

With it out of the way, Torrence dropped to her knees and used her hands to search the snow for her weapon. Finding it, she stood and then used the heads-up, but the only shapes she saw were human.

Over the short-com, she said, "Let's fall back. Regroup. Ramey, give us a signal."

"Yes, ma'am." Ramey started a short count.

Torrence knew they were violating a dozen radio procedures, but at the moment, she didn't care. All she wanted to do was get the majority of the company reorganized.

She pushed her way through the snow, searching for the rest of the soldiers. Using the heads-up, she spotted a group of them and angled toward them.

She reached Ramey and sank to her knees, letting the snow cushion her. To him, she said, "What's our status?"

"We've got five dead, a dozen missing and about twice that many wounded, and we haven't done shit."

Torrence checked the time. The second wave would be launched at any moment, and they had yet to destroy a single defensive position on the ground.

Jefferson had moved from the bridge to his command post set up in the intelligence office. He stood near the bulkhead where he could see the flatscreens and watch as the technicians worked.

Carter saw him enter, nodded, and then turned back to his work. Facing the radio console in front of him, he said, "We seem to have fallen behind schedule."

Jefferson pushed himself away from the bulkhead and asked, "Why do you say that?"

Carter pointed to the main flatscreen, touched a button and watched as a map of the industrial complex came up. "There has been no change there since the first wave landed."

"You're sure?"

"We'd have seen nothing."

Jefferson knew what he meant. There were to be no radio signals of any kind, but if there was a major change in any of the ground targets, the various instruments should be able to detect it.

"They're down, aren't they?" asked Jefferson.

"Yes, sir. We watched the deployment right here. Nothing to it. Disappeared into the clouds."

"Regular clouds?" asked Jefferson.

"Seem to be the same kind of clouds we've seen on a dozen other planets. Just like those we see on the Earth. Nothing strange about them."

Jefferson was thinking about a company of soldiers that had disappeared while being watched on various instruments. Nothing left but an ionization trail and then a ship that had been masked by a satellite.

"You getting anything at all?" he asked.

"Nothing, General. Just the normal background that we'd expect."

"Can you pinpoint the landing sites?"

"Certainly, but that's going to require an output of energy that will be fairly easy for them to detect."

"Do it."

"Yes, General." Carter leaned over his console, touched a few of the buttons and then said, "Clarke, come up on the sensor board."

"Roger that."

The scene on the flatscreen changed again. Carter studied it for a second and said, "Pods are down."

"Cut the probe," said Jefferson.

"Probing has been cut," said Clarke.

"Can you tell me anything else?" asked Jefferson.

"I can make a probe into the city proper," said Carter, "but there are going to be telltale signs. If they're looking, they'll know that someone is probing, and they'll be able to trace it back to us, here."

"In a couple of hours they're going to be well aware of it," said Jefferson. "Do it."

"On the center screen," Carter said.

Jefferson moved around so that he was standing in front of the screen. He watched as the electronic display, enhanced by computer discrimination, focused on the center screen.

"We've got movement down there," said Carter. "Hey, here's something."

"What?"

"Ambient temperature is running about minus four Celisus. Colder than I thought."

"You've got our people spotted?" asked Jefferson. He was studying one of the screens.

"See the moving dots? Those are warm-blooded creatures. Track seems to be from the pod landing sites toward the defensive ring around the city. The only possible conclusion is that it'll be our people."

"They're short of their targets," said Jefferson.

"Yes, General, which explains why we haven't got any indications of their success."

"I've got to deploy the second wave in about twenty minutes," said Jefferson.

Carter turned in his seat and faced the general. "All I can tell you is that there is no indication the enemy knows we're down there."

Jefferson studied the screen for several seconds, unaware of the others standing around him. He ignored the quiet hissing, popping and pinging of the electronic gear. He ignored the quiet talk of the technicians as they watched the scene on their equipment.

"Carter," he said finally, "call control and tell them to hold the second wave for twenty minutes."

"Yes, General. What are you going to do?"

"Give our people a little extra time to accomplish their missions."

"Yes, sir."

"Anything changes down there, you let me know immediately. You get any indication that the enemy has spotted our people, you let me know."

"Yes, General."

Jefferson moved to the hatch and then stopped before leaving. "I'll be in the control room if you have anything for me."

"Yes, sir."

Jefferson left then, feeling that he'd just thrown away another regiment. There was definitely something wrong on the ground.

13

CLEMENS DIDN'T THINK they'd get into action this time. There were too many other ships, and there were too many soldiers who would be landing on the planet's surface. If the enemy was there, they'd be busy protecting their home world. They wouldn't be worrying about a fleet so far from their planet. That had been Clemens' thinking.

"Captain, we've lost contact with Delta Four."

"Plot that on the screen please," said Clemens.

"Aye, Captain."

The screen focused on the gas giant again. The location of Delta Four began to flash.

"Give me the location of the other lost picket."

It came up a moment later. Clemens sat bolt upright and yelled, "Full battle alert now!"

There was a moment of quiet and then a sudden buzzing that filled the bridge. A female voice said, "Battle stations. Battle stations. Battle stations."

Clemens slammed a fist into the control button on the side of his chair. "Surveillance."

"Surveillance, aye."

"Full sweep of our starboard beam at full power. Everything you have."

"Surveillance, aye."

"Plot," said Clemens.

"Plot, aye."

"Give everything you have to Targeting. Last known locations of the two missing pickets, their patrol paths and their last observations."

"Plot, aye."

"Targeting?"

"Targeting, aye."

"You monitor that?"

"Targeting, aye. We've monitored all that. Weapons systems are set and ready."

"Stand by," said Clemens. He turned to the men and women on the bridge with him. "Anything?"

"No, Captain. Screens, sensors and radars are all clear," said the Intelligence Officer.

"Any indication of what might have happened to those two scouts?"

"Negative, Captain."

Clemens turned back to the screen and searched it with his eyes, knowing there was nothing he would be able to see that the instruments wouldn't have detected minutes earlier. The warning would have already been issued if there had been anything there.

It was maddening to be stuck sitting in the chair. He wanted to *do* something himself. Use the instruments to find the enemy. He wanted to give orders to attack them, but there was no one to attack. Just two picket ships that had vanished while on what was supposed to be a routine patrol.

"Bridge, Surveillance."

"Go," said Clemens.

"We've got a motion-detection out here, but it doesn't seem to be a very large craft." The voice was different from the first one. Clemens didn't recognize it.

"On the main screen," said Clemens.

"It's centered there now, Captain."

Clemens stared at it. "I see nothing there."

"Merely motion-detection."

"Targeting," said Clemens.

"Targeting, aye."

"Give me a spread of four torpedoes into the center of the disturbance that Surveillance has reported."

"Targeting, aye." There was a moment's hesitation and then, "Targeting ready."

"You may fire."

They heard nothing when the torpedoes were fired. Just the quiet voice of the Targeting officer. "Torpedoes away. Six minutes to impact."

Clemens leaned forward, an elbow on his knee as he stared at the screen in front of him. He still could see nothing that could be causing the motion.

"Three minutes," said Targeting.

"Plot," said Clemens. "You have anything new?"

"Plot, negative, Captain. We're continuing to monitor the situation."

"Surveillance?" asked Clemens.

"Surveillance, negative. We're still searching but have found nothing else."

"One minute," said Targeting.

"Magnification ten on center screen," said Clemens. "Be prepared to dim."

"Aye aye, Captain."

"Thirty seconds."

Now, with the magnification increased, Clemens could see the tiny rocket engines of the torpedoes as they burned in the blackness of space. He couldn't spot the target but he knew that something was out there.

There was a sudden flare as one of the torpedoes detonated. The expanding cloud seemed to engulf a second torpedo causing it to explode. The other two held in space a moment longer and then they too were destroyed.

"Surveillance?"

"It's still there, Captain."

"You have a size on it?"

"Negative. Our readings don't make any sense. It's either very tiny or it's extremely large. We're still working on the problem."

"Targeting, did you score a hit?"

"Negative, Captain. Our torpedoes detonated more than a thousand klicks short of the target."

"Targeting," said Clemens, "I want to use our missiles this time."

"Targeting is ready."

"Fire," said Clemens.

"Missiles away."

"Give me a second spread," said Clemens.

"Missiles away."

He watched as they entered the screen and began a rapid cocksrew pattern designed to defeat enemy anti-missile defenses.

"One minute to impact,"

Clemens kept his eyes on the center of the screen, waiting. The missiles left short tracks, looking almost like little beams from lasers.

"Thirty seconds."

One of the missiles exploded, and the others changed their evasive pattern, two of them looking as if they were breaking away from the attack. A second blew up, but the others continued to fly.

"Going to get him this time," said Clemens.

There was a single, fiery detonation. The outline of a ship flared in bright orange-yellow that burned out suddenly. It was a brilliant flash of light that was gone immediately.

"That hurt him," yelled one of the officers on the bridge, slamming a hand to his console.

"Surveillance, can you give me a look at him?" asked Clemens.

"Computer-generated display coming up now, Captain. Left screen."

The ship was long and thin, looking like a small cigar. There were no fins on it, no ports, no hatches, and there didn't seem to be any engines. There was nothing on the surface of it at all.

"Jesus, they've taken the stealth technology to the extreme," someone said.

"Surveillance, you get anything from their engines? Any heat detections?"

"Negative, Captain. They've got that well masked. All we picked up was the motion."

"Let's sweep completely around that ship then," said Clemens.

"Aye, Captain."

"Communications," said Clemens. "Report this to the other battleships and have them initiate their own search patterns using that enemy as the base."

"Aye, Captain."

"Bridge, we've got something coming around the gas giant now. Motion-detection."

"Targeting."

"This is Targeting. We monitored that and have it sighted in."

"Captain, it looks like that first ship is beginning to move again."

"Targeting," said Clemens.

"We have it locked in. Do you want us to fire again?"

Clemens turned his attention to the screen but didn't see a thing. He glanced to the left at the computer display model that was turning slowly. It didn't look like a warship, but it had taken the barrage of the missiles, and it had destroyed the spread of torpedoes.

"Surveillance, can we get a new look at the enemy ship?" asked Clemens.

"We're trying everything, Captain. We're beginning to pick up something in the infrared band but at low levels. We might have damaged it."

"Put it on the computer."

"Aye, sir."

"Captain, we've just lost another of the pickets," said an officer.

"On the main screen."

Now the view shifted slightly. Clemens was no longer looking at the gaseous giant. He was staring out of the system in the direction they had come from.

"Nothing there," said Clemens.

"Got motion back there. Signature is the same as the ship we fired on."

"Understood," said Clemens.

"Bridge, Targeting. We're ready to fire."

"Wait one," said Clemens. "Communications, alert Captains Knight and Fogel that we've got an enemy ship to our stern. Ask them if they are prepared to take it under fire."

"Aye, Captain." There was a moment's hesitation and then, "Captains Knight and Fogel report they have spotted the target and are prepared to engage."

"Targeting, you may fire on my mark. Communications, please advise the captains to fire at will."

"Communications, aye."

"Targeting, you may fire."

"Targeting, aye."

This time the spread of missiles and torpedoes was larger than it had been the first time. They raced toward the rear of the fleet, the torpedoes running straight and true and the missiles dodging and weaving like a prize fighter in the ring.

"One minute to contact."

It seemed that space lit up then. The first of the torpedoes detonated, followed closely by a number of the missiles that were engulfed in the fire cloud.

"Targeting," said Clemens, his voice rising slightly. "Can you hit them with your beams?"

"We can try it, Captain. They're at the extreme range at the moment."

"Do so," said Clemens.

Now the beamed weapons flashed out, joining the racing missiles and torpedoes. The beams struck first, dancing across the invisible surface of the enemy ships. There were flares of brightness and a dull cherry glow that began along the hull of the ship.

"Got a computer model," said one of the officers.

"On the screen."

It was a new ship, longer, fatter, bigger than the others. There were fins at both ends. The computer showed nothing that could be considered weapons. The craft was headed straight at them.

"Targeting," said Clemens. "You are cleared to destroy the enemy ship."

"Targeting, aye."

"Communications, please inform Captains Knight and Fogel that we must destroy the enemy ship."

"Communications, aye."

Clemens wiped a hand over his face, surprised to find it sweaty. He glanced at his wet fingers and then rubbed them on the chest of his uniform. He felt the tension build as he waited for someone else to do something.

The center of the screen flared suddenly. A bright light that wiped out all other images and then slowly faded. Clemens was on his feet.

"What was that?"

"Plot here, Captain. I think we've just lost the *Roland Stone*."

"Communications, get me the captain of the *Stone*."

"Nothing there, Captain."

"Plot?"

"We've lost all contact with the ship."

Clemens turned his attention back to the main screen. The missiles were beginning to detonate, some of them a thousand klicks or more from the enemy vessel, but others were getting through the defenses.

"She's firing on us," shouted an officer.

"Helm, accelerate."

"Accelerating, Captain."

"Communications, have all ship's captains maneuver for the safety of their ships. We will cover the troop transports as they begin their assault runs."

"Aye, Captain."

Clemens now kept his eyes clued to the center of the screen. He watched the sudden twinkling of space, looking as if all the fireflies on Earth had escaped. Those were the flashes of the enemy's weapons.

"Missiles coming in," said the Intelligence Officer.

"Targeting?"

"Aye, Captain. We have them and are firing on them."

As the Targeting Officer spoke, the first of the enemy missiles detonated. It was a dull flash on the right side of the screen.

"Bridge, Targeting. That was fairly low yield. I doubt it would have disrupted our screens."

"Surveillance, can you give me a reading on the enemy missiles?"

"Wait one."

Two more of the missiles disappeared from the screen. Neither created much in the way of a flash of light or radiation. Both had been low yield.

"Captain, Surveillance. These are little more than bullets. Not much explosive force when they detonate. They rely on kinetic energy for their destructive force. We should be able to absorb them if they get through our screens."

"Targeting, did you monitor?"

"Targeting, aye."

Clemens stared at the screen and then remembered the first ship. "Surveillance, do you still have a fix on the first target?"

"Aye, Skipper. It's dead in space now. It hasn't moved in twelve minutes."

"If it does, please let me know."

"Surveillance, aye."

Now he focused on the second enemy ship. He watched as the beams danced across the hull and as the missiles dived in, detonating against it.

The enemy's missiles raced at him, but Targeting took them out one by one, killing the closest of them first. It wasn't much in the way of an attack.

More of his weapons appeared, diving at the enemy ship that was now visible thanks to the glowing of its hull. Beams struck it repeatedly and now the missiles and torpedoes were falling on it, exploding against the metal. Internal fires were burning, causing the ship to superheat.

"Looks like he's dying," said the Intelligence Officer.

Clemens didn't want to encourage that. He wanted everyone to work until they knew the enemy was dead. That was the only way to win the war.

A moment later the enemy ship seemed to shudder and began to collapse in on itself. Fire flared from both ends and then out of a hole that exploded into the center of it. Debris no longer hidden by the stealth capabilities began to fly off, and a moment later, the whole ship disintegrated.

Cheering erupted on the bridge. Two officers grabbed one another and danced around, screaming.

"Knock it off," snapped Clemens. "We're not out of the woods yet."

Then, almost as if to prove his point, the Communications Officer said, "Captain, Captain Knight reports that he is under heavy attack."

"On the screen."

Missiles and torpedoes seemed to materialize out of space. There didn't seem to be anything behind them.

"Targeting, can you assist Knight?"

"Negative, Captain. We've got everything committed to the fight behind us. Besides, the range is too great for us to do anything effectively."

"Communications, have Captain Negev assist Knight."

"Aye, Captain."

Clemens watched the fighting on the flatscreen in front of him. It was almost like watching a computer game of his youth. There was nothing to suggest that the ships and weapons were any more real than those created in the microchip memory of a video game. Real people were hidden by the electronic images, and yet Clemens didn't think of them as real. They were electronically generated ships that he had to destroy or lose the game.

"Targeting," he said.

"Targeting, aye."

"How are you doing? Give me a weapons status."

"We're down five percent on the missiles, less than two percent on the torpedoes and both particle and laser weapons remain fully charged."

Clemens stepped back and then sat down on his chair. For the first time in an hour he began to relax. It didn't seem that the enemy had invented anything new.

14

JEFFERSON FOUND HIS deputy commander, Colonel William Bowen, standing at the hatch to the drop bay. Bowen was an old man by the brigade's standards. Pushing forty, he had been in the Army for over twenty years. But those who knew him couldn't believe that he was that old. They guessed his age at thirty-two or thirty-three, depending on the lighting, the time of day and Bowen's mood. He was a tall, slender man who was in good physical shape with only a hint of gray hair that was impossible to see right after a haircut. He tried to keep it trimmed short.

"I'm going down," said Jefferson.

Bowen turned and looked at the general. "As the commander, you should remain on board. Command and control is easier up here."

"The commanding general should be with the soldiers," said Jefferson.

"The commanding general should be where it is easiest for him to keep track of the brigade."

"Colonel, I don't need you to tell me where I belong. The troops on the ground expect to see the general down there with them. They don't want him to remain here, on board with air conditioning, hot meals and mostly hot water, while they're on the ground getting their butts shot off."

"It makes no difference what the troops want," said Bowen. "The general must do what is best for the brigade."

"The general," said Jefferson, stressing the words, "must do what the general wants."

"Yes, General."

"I'm going down. You can coordinate from up here. I expect you stay in the Intell Office and watch everything. But I'm going down."

"Yes, General."

He turned and let the hatch iris open. He stepped through. Inside the shuttle bay he found preparations to drop the second regiment were nearly completed. Everything was right on schedule.

Jefferson pushed forward and found the regiment's commander, Colonel Richard Peel standing near the command ring. He was yelling at a sailor. Screaming at him in a voice so high and thin it was impossible to understand him.

"What the hell?" asked Jefferson as he walked up.

Peel whirled, looking as if he was going to kill whoever was interrupting, and then recognized Jefferson. He stood for a moment but said nothing.

"What's going on?"

The sailor started to speak, but Peel cut him off. "You don't say a word unless I tell you to."

"Aye aye, sir."

"And stop that 'aye aye' crap. You answer like a human being or you keep your mouth shut."

Jefferson shot a glance at the sailor, a young man whose face had drained of color and who looked as if he were about to be hanged.

"Colonel Peel," said Jefferson. "Might I have a word with you?"

"Certainly, General," said Peel, suddenly calm. To the sailor, he added, "You wait right here. I'm not through with you."

"Aye . . . I mean, yes, sir."

Jefferson moved away from the sailor and then lowered his

voice. "What in the hell are you doing? You've no right to berate a sailor like that."

"Sailor? That idiot was supposed to replace a single video terminal in the command pod, but he short-circuited the electronics in the whole thing. Burned the interior up. It's useless to us now."

"He do it on purpose?" asked Jefferson.

"No. The man's an idiot. A jerk who wouldn't be worth his weight in garbage."

"And you've never made a mistake," said Jefferson reasonably.

"Don't pull that bullshit on me," said Peel. "I won't fall for it."

"Fine," said Jefferson, his voice rising slightly. "And don't you take that tone with me, Colonel."

"I've been a regimental commander in this division for six years," said Peel.

"You keep talking to me like that and you'll find yourself without a job."

Peel stood staring into Jefferson's eyes for an instant. Then suddenly he said, "Yes, General."

Jefferson shook his head. "Don't you remember how it was when you were a new second lieutenant and couldn't find your ass with both hands and a road map?"

"The point here, General, is that he's supposed to be trained. He's supposed to be qualified. He's not supposed to destroy equipment."

"I thought I made it clear," said Jefferson, "that the discussion was over. I don't ever want to see you treating a sailor or a soldier like that again. You do and you'll be looking for a new job. Do I make myself clear?"

"Yes, General."

"Now, I'm going to deploy with your regiment. Once on the ground, I'll be trying to link up with Torrence, and once the last regiment is down, I'll establish the brigade's headquarters in the rear of Torrence's regiment."

"Yes, General. Will you require an escort?"

"No. I'll have the headquarters company deploy with me. They'll serve as the escort."

CHAIN OF COMMAND

"Certainly, General. Will that be in addition to the units of my regiment?"

Jefferson thought for a moment. The schedule didn't call for him to deploy at that moment. Slipping his headquarters company into the deployment could create a problem for Peel if he ran into stiff resistance.

"I'll check with control and see if they can add us to the manifest for this drop. If not, I'll drop with a single platoon and we'll try to stay out of your way."

"Yes, General. If that's all, I'll get with my battalion commanders and alert them to the change."

"You do that," said Jefferson.

As Peel walked off, Bowen moved forward and said quietly, "Peel's just become your enemy."

"Colonel, I don't worry about subordinates who think of me as their enemy. I'll bet twenty-five percent of the brigade believes that I'm the enemy. Right now we have other problems. But if I find that Peel is acting out of his own self-interest, I'll nail his ass to a board."

"Yes, General."

"Get with Captain James and have him prepare to deploy to the planet's surface."

"Yes, sir."

Jefferson walked across the deck to the control booth. He found the officer of the deck standing near it, a mini-computer held in his left hand. To the man Jefferson said, "What is the status of the pods?"

"Ready for regimental deployment. Only need to load the soldiers and then hit the line of departure."

"How long?"

"Twenty minutes from now." He glanced up at Jefferson. "Give or take a couple of minutes."

"Can you accommodate an additional company?"

The man touched the buttons on his mini-computer, read the words that crawled across the miniature screen and shook his head. "We'll be about thirty pods short."

"Okay, I want one additional platoon ready to deploy with the regiment."

"Certainly, General, that'll be no problem."

"Oh, Colonel Peel jumped all over one of your sailors. See that the sailor learns that Colonel Peel was out of line without making the colonel look like too much of a jackass if that's possible."

"Certainly."

Cooper found himself standing in the basement of the building. It looked like a conventional basement, open from one end to the other with supports spread throughout so the building wouldn't collapse in on itself. For a moment he stood there, feeling like he'd stumbled into something that belonged on Earth and wondering if it was a nightmare induced by too much pizza and beer in the ship's cantina.

Franz ran up behind him, stopped and started. "What in the hell?"

"Basement," said Cooper.

"I thought we'd find the equipment. Generators or radios or something down here."

As she spoke, Cooper realized what was wrong. The basement was too open and clean. It wasn't like those on Earth used for storage and for the heavy equipment that would run the rest of the building's machinery. It wasn't filled with broken furniture and other rubbish.

"If we cut the supports," said Cooper, "wouldn't that drop everything into the basement? That would take this structure out of the fight."

"How long to wire it?" asked Franz.

"Full squad, probably no more then fifteen minutes. Hell, we don't have to be clever about it. Just cut all the supports and the building will self-destruct. It'll collapse on itself when the supports are gone."

"Do it," said Franz.

Cooper turned and saw two other squad members. "You two head across the floor and begin wiring the supports. Set them so that you blow a chunk out of them."

Franz said, "I'll take Haggerson. We'll set up the machine-gun in the corridor to defend in case there's a push by the enemy."

Cooper ran across the floor, realizing that it wasn't concrete

CHAIN OF COMMAND 113

as he had expected. It was something softer, warmer, more like astroturf. The enemy apparently didn't like naked concrete.

He stooped near one of the support beams. It looked smaller than he expected. The surface was smooth and squared and didn't look like ordinary steel.

Cooper pulled some explosive from his pouch, slapped it onto the beam and then molded it so that it would cut through the metal. Finished. He moved to the next one, did the same and continued until he was out of explosive. He then pushed a detonator into the explosive and retraced his steps, playing out the det cord. When he finished, he joined the others who had completed their tasks.

Franz was watching from the corridor. She shouted, "Let's get going. We're almost on time here."

All the members of the squad converged on the corridor. Cooper took their det cords and wired them together. "I can explode it electronically, time it or we can light the fuse and run like hell."

"Time it," said Franz. "Ten minutes. That should give us time to get the hell out."

Cooper did as he was told and then said, "That's got it."

"So let's get the hell out of here," yelled Franz. Her voice was a little high.

They sprinted up the corridor, running for the door they had used to enter the basement. Haggerson got there first and threw it open. She then leaped back to cover the others as they ran out.

As the first of the men ran through the door, there was a crackling in the air and a bright green beam slashed through it. The man took the beam full in the chest, but his uniform absorbed the energy from it.

"They've got us trapped," he yelled as he dived back in.

Haggerson fired through the door, the machine-gun hammering, the huge slugs ripping through the corridor.

"How long?" asked Franz.

"Six minutes," said Cooper.

Two of the men pushed their way forward and began firing out the door. The beams of their weapons flashed into the darkness of the room beyond them.

"Five minutes," said Cooper.

"Grenades," said Franz. "On my mark. And then we attack on through."

"Got it," said Cooper.

"Ready?" said Franz. "Ready. And. Mark."

The grenades arched through the door. The beamed weapons of the enemy opened fire. They punched through the walls and tore up the floor, leaving steaming, glowing paths. Cooper was touched briefly, but his uniform absorbed the energy, channeling it into his powerpack.

A moment later the grenades detonated with reverberating bangs. As they did, Franz screamed, "Let's go."

The squad charged through the door and into the room beyond it. As they did, the enemy began to shoot. Beams sliced through the air. One soldier slipped, and the enemy fired at him, their beams hitting him repeatedly. The powerpack began to whine was it overloaded. He grabbed at it, trying to rip it away. The whine increased to a wail.

"Help me," he screamed.

Cooper opened fire, raking the far side of the room with his laser. The beam slashed at the wall, melting part of it, but the enemy kept firing at the downed man who was trying to scramble clear.

The wailing of the powerpack had become a banshee scream. The man was yanking at his side, trying to get rid of the powerpack before it exploded. The enemy beams were playing across him. One of them slashed his eyes and the man screamed again, suddenly blind, no longer worried about the powerpack.

"It's going up," yelled Franz as she dived to the side.

There was an explosion and the screaming stopped.

Cooper rolled to his right, spotted one of the enemy and fired at him. The beam seemed to reflect from the enemy's clothes. It fired back at him.

"How long?" asked Franz.

Cooper had forgotten about the explosives in the basement. They had to be running out of time. Without answering, he yelled, "Cover me."

Firing erupted all around the room. The brightly colored

beams, reds, greens and pale blues flashed, creating the illusion of a multicolored net over them.

Cooper crawled back toward the door. He was going to stop the explosion and give them a chance to get out. He reached the door, leaped through it and rolled up against the wall. He struggled to his feet, keeping his back against the smooth material of the wall.

He risked a glance at his watch and realized he would never make it. Only seconds remained. And then he heard the first of the explosions. It was a muffled bang, followed by another and another until it was one long drawn-out detonation. Overhead he could hear the building beginning to creak and groan as the weight-bearing beams were cut.

Spinning, Cooper ran back through the door. "We've got to get out—*now!*" he yelled. He didn't stop, but ran for the door at the other end of the room, ignoring the enemy soldiers and the firing.

He dived at the door and hit it low, his shoulder slamming into it. He heard bones pop and felt pain shoot through his upper chest. For a moment he thought he was going to be sick and then ignored the feelings. He tried to roll over and out into the snow-choked night.

There were more detonations in the building, but these were from the last of the load-bearing walls collapsing. The whole building began to groan as the floors caved in.

Cooper, unaware of what was happening behind him, struggled to his feet and staggered away from the building. He fell into the snow and couldn't move. There was too much pain in his shoulder, and his muscles refused to work.

Behind him, one more person escaped from the building before it crumpled. The walls fell in and there was a loud crashing as the building destroyed itself.

Cooper finally rolled to his back and then sat up. He groaned in pain, felt suddenly lightheaded and thought he was going to faint. He saw a shape loom out of the swirling, blowing snow and thought the enemy had found him. Halfheartedly, he reached for his weapon, but he'd lost it in the scramble to get out of the building.

The shape staggered closer and then dropped to its knees near him. Cooper couldn't recognize it until it spoke.

"Well," said Franz, "we succeeded. We destroyed the target."

Cooper nodded once, felt a flash of pain and then asked, "At what price?"

15

TORRENCE HAD LED the charge, though it wasn't much of an attack. Two hundred soldiers, struggling through thigh-deep snow as they headed for a cluster of buildings that might have been designed as defensive installations. Torrence didn't know the real purpose of the buildings and didn't care. Intelligence had labeled them as defensive and it was her job to see that they were knocked out.

They had assembled in a snow-choked ditch about fifty meters from the side of one of the buildings. Torrence had used her heads-up and then the image enhancer to inspect the target. There didn't seem to be any heat sources in it, no signs of activity or life, and no indication that it was anything that could attack the fleet. However, Torrence wasn't there to judge the value of the target, she was there to eliminate it.

Satisfied that she'd located the correct complex, she slipped back down into the narrow ditch, nearly disappearing in the deep snow. She used the short-com. "All officers report to me."

Ramey and Crowley were the first there, followed by the platoon leaders and then two staff officers. Torrence looked at each of them and then said, "We've got the target spotted. No sign of activity. We advance slowly, leap-frogging forward with the first platoon leading the way. Once there, we split up, one platoon to a building. We have twelve minutes to complete the task."

"We're not going to make it in less than twelve minutes," said Ramey.

"I know that," said Torrence. "I was just letting you know the situation so that you'll hurry."

"Yes, ma'am."

"If there are no questions, let's get going."

The officers scattered, pushing their way through the blowing snow, rejoining their units. Torrence scrambled back out of the ditch and crouched on the edge of it, looking back at the complex of buildings.

Over the short-com, she heard, "Command, this is First. We're ready."

"Call in platoon order."

"One, set."

"Second is ready."

"Three is a go."

"Four is set."

Torrence cut in and said, "Let's go."

There was no response, and in the blinding snowstorm, she wasn't sure that anyone would be out there with her. It might be just her and four or five others rushing to a quick death. But she was up and moving, leaning into the wind and trying to see what was ten feet in front of her. The enemy installation loomed over them, barely visible in the storm.

She reached a wall and stopped, taking cover in the shelter of it. Out of the wind, it seemed almost warm. She raised a hand and rubbed the snow from her eyes.

"Now what?" asked a soldier.

"We get inside it. Find us a door or blow a hole in the wall."

"Yes, ma'am."

Torrence checked the time again and saw that only four minutes remained. The enemy's war-making capability was supposed to have been decreased by then. And his installations were supposed to have been destroyed by then. That had been the original plan.

Silently she said, "Sorry, David. I just couldn't get it done. It's this damned snowstorm."

Over the short-com, she heard. "Got a door open."

"Where are you?"

"Center of the wall."

Torrence wasn't sure where the center of the wall was. She thought it was to the left and started working her way along it until she saw a group of soldiers standing around.

As she approached, she demanded, "What in the hell are you people doing?"

Before anyone could answer, the enemy came boiling out the door. A dozen or more of them, screaming in high-pitched voices. They were waving weapons, firing into the sky. Beams of orange, red and yellow flashed and then reflected on the snow.

Torrence fired from the hip, her ruby-colored beam slicing through one of the enemy soldiers. It fell into the snow, losing the grip on its own weapon.

Torrence turned to face another and was hit by a beam. She felt the heat of it on her chest and dodged to the right, away from it. She fired back but missed.

Something hit her in the back, and she fell to her knees, losing her grip on her rifle. She reached back and grabbed a handful of material. She dropped her shoulder as she pulled, yanking the creature there from her. It landed on its side, the fall cushioned by the deep snow. Torrence punched once and struck it in the side of the head. The bone there gave slightly but didn't crack or break.

The creature grabbed her hand and tried to drag her forward, but Torrence resisted. She suddenly fell forward, smashing an elbow into the face of the creature. She heard the satisfying sound of bone breaking and the sudden scream of the alien. It bucked once, trying to throw her off.

Torrence reached out and grabbed her knife. She slashed at the creature, the sharp blade cutting through the soft flesh. Blood of some kind burst from the body, and the air was filled with a foul stench. Torrence turned her head to the side and tried to find some fresh air.

The being stopped moving then and lay still behind her.

Torrence pushed herself up and took a step back, away from the creature. She sheathed her knife and bent to pick up her rifle.

Around her the fighting had ended. The enemy were all dead. Two of her soldiers lay in the snow. Another leaned against the side of the building holding his side.

Glancing at her watch, she saw that time had expired. The second wave was coming in and as far as she could tell, she and the regiment had not captured a single objective. The enemy's defensive installations were all still intact.

Jefferson had no indication that he was about to fall into a blizzard. The numbers on the heads-up display inside his pod told him that it was going to be chilly, and he knew it was overcast, but there was nothing to tell him about the snow. It was a fact that had gone unreported.

Using the intelligence channel, Jefferson reviewed the information they had received. Enemy installations that were supposed to have been attacked and eliminated were still up and running, but there was no indication they were firing on the assault troops.

Jefferson shifted slightly and pushed another button. There were also no indications that Torrence's regiment had run into any real trouble. None of the transponders, none of the emergency circuits and none of the desperation channels had been opened. As far as he could tell, Torrence and her troops were on the ground and making progress. But they had failed in accomplishing most of their mission in the allotted time.

Jefferson felt the chutes deploy and the rockets fire. The numbers of the altimeter slowed as they approached the ground. There wasn't much of a jolt as he touched down. He hit the release and the lid of the pod popped open.

As soon as it did, Jefferson, looking out on the snow field, said, "Son of a bitch." He pushed himself free of the pod and sank into the snow. He struggled to turn around and was hit in the face by a blast of icy air.

Peel came up and saluted. "Regiment is down, General. We're ready to move."

"Do it," said Jefferson. He moved away from Peel and

found Lieutenant Arney. The lieutenant was crouched near his pod, an ear cocked so that he could listen to the radios in it, but no one was broadcasting.

"You ready, Lieutenant?" asked Jefferson.

"Certainly, General."

"Then let's move out. I want to sweep around to the left and link up with Colonel Torrence."

"Yes, sir. You know where she is?"

Jefferson grinned. "I know where she's supposed to be. That's as good as it gets."

"Yes, General." Arney stood up and waved an arm. "Let's saddle up and get ready to move."

Jefferson stood for a moment and looked up at the sky. Snow was continuing to fall. It wouldn't take long for it to drift and hide most of the equipment. Evidence of the landing would be gone in an hour or two.

Jefferson didn't wait for Arney to find him again. He joined the platoon, taking a position in the center of the line. He nodded at the platoon leader and said, "You've got it, Lieutenant."

"Yes, sir." He turned and took his first step. The rest of the platoon fell in behind him.

Jefferson, holding his rifle in both hands, tried to see through the curtain of snow. He took a step forward, stopped and then began to move quickly.

The line of soldiers hurried forward, skirting the edge of the city. Jefferson could almost make it out through the snow. He was aware of it without seeing much of it.

Arney let his senior NCO take the point and slipped back to where Jefferson was. To the general, he said, "There doesn't seem to be much activity."

Jefferson nodded. "If we were on Earth and had this snowstorm going, we'd know that the enemy is close. We'd be out searching for them, trying to eliminate them."

"Maybe we caught them totally off guard," said Arney hopefully.

"They have to know we're here. Hell, we're talking about a race that travels in space. A little snow is not going to blind their radars and sensors."

"Then where are they?" asked Arney.

Jefferson reached up with his right hand and brushed the snow from his face. "That's a hell of a good question."

They walked on in silence for a few moments. Jefferson turned to the right where he could barely see the glow of the city through the blizzard. It was a warm yellow glow, marking the electric lights.

On Earth, the simple radars of War Two had been defeated easily. But within a couple of years, they had developed to the point where they could "see" rainfall or snowfall or be set so they saw neither. They had all-weather radar that wasn't useless in bad weather. A race that could travel through space had to have developed the equipment that would let them detect the enemy as it drew near regardless of the weather on the planet, the solar activity or the problems caused by hydrogen storms in space.

Jefferson found the walking difficult. The wind was so strong that it threatened to knock the soldiers from their feet. The snow was blowing so hard that at times it was impossible to see anything. The men and women stopped, waited for the wind to let up, and then pushed on.

Arney moved closer again, and over the sound of the wind, said, "There should have been a counterattack by now. They should have reacted."

"Yes," agreed Jefferson. He knew there hadn't been. Even if Torrence had not been able to tell him that, there would have been detectable indications of it. There was nothing to suggest that the enemy had tried to stop the landings, had tried to wipe out the first regiment or that they even knew that the second and third had landed.

"I don't like this," said Arney.

Jefferson knew what he was saying. It seemed that the enemy was letting them walk into a trap. He was letting the people from Earth land, move into the city and then would strike back. It wasn't a military tactic that Jefferson would have used, but then there was no way to guess what the alien mind would come up with.

"Once we find Colonel Torrence," said Jefferson, "we'll have a better feel for what is going on down here."

"If they don't do something soon, it's going to be too late to act."

The wind picked up again, the gusts coming in a rhythm that seemed designed to make walking as difficult as possible. Jefferson slipped to one knee, ducked his head and waited until the wind died down a little.

"Jesus," said Arney. "You'd have thought that intelligence would have been able to tell us it was snowing."

"Not their job," said Jefferson.

"I beg to differ, General. It's their job to provide us with all the information we need to complete our tasks. Weather comes under that heading. They should have known."

Jefferson nodded and then said, "Let's find Colonel Torrence."

"Maybe we should contact the fleet," said Arney. "Maybe we should get the hell out of here until we find out what's going on."

For a moment Jefferson considered the idea and then shook his head. "We're not going to abandon the assault until there is a real reason to do it. Keep the people moving."

"Yes, General."

Jefferson watched as Arney vanished into the snow again. He was beginning to feel the panic that was infecting the rest of the troops. Everyone wanted to get out of the snow and off the enemy's planet, and the enemy had yet to put in a real appearance. Jefferson thought about that and decided that if he ever had to defend a planet, he'd remember the tactic. Let the enemy scare themselves into retreating.

16

CARSON DIDN'T SEE where the shot came from. It was a beam that seemed to come out of space, rake across the side of his ship and then disappear. Carson pushed the control yoke forward to accelerate and then twisted it to the right so he could begin a spiraling turn to take him out of the line of fire.

Twisting and turning in his seat, trying to see back over his shoulder, trying to get something on the screen, Carson fought to get away, though he didn't know from what. Out of the corner of his eye, a bluish beam flashed past, looking like a meteor seen on a dark night on Earth.

Carson flipped the yoke to the other side and pulled it back as far as he could. The nose came up, rolled over to the left, and he began another tight turn. He pushed it forward suddenly and the nose dropped, pushing the tiny scout ship in a new direction.

And still he couldn't see the enemy ship. It had to be a ship because the shot had not come from the direction of the planet. If it had, he would have seen it, even if it had been only a beamed weapon.

Carson flipped the yoke again and began a three-hundred-sixty-degree turn. There was nothing around him except the blackness of space, a sprinkling of stars and a couple of planets.

He looped the ship then, giving him another all-around view, but there was nothing to see in space near him. And the attack had stopped just as quickly as it had begun. Nothing was firing at him now.

Carson used the radio. "Savage Six, Savage Six, this is Scout Four."

There was a delay caused by the distance and then a warning. "Four, you are to remain silent."

Carson had to smile at that. Typical of the military mind. If he was ordered to remain silent, then he must do so, regardless of what he had learned. Only those on the ship were smart enough to break radio silence.

"Six, be advised that I have been attacked by an unseen ship."

"Four, stand by."

That was the last thing Carson was going to do. He'd not seen any activity on the planet's surface that suggested any type of enemy resistance. He accelerated along a straight line, seeming to dive at the planet's surface and then turned again, pushing for more forward speed. He was slung away from the planet's surface.

Firing from the unseen and undetected enemy came again. There were missiles that didn't have the speed to catch him. And there were beams, some of which brushed across his ship, scorching it but doing no real damage.

"Four, say location."

Carson laughed out loud. That was the dumbest thing he'd heard yet. They were supposed to know his location, and even though he'd abandoned his post over the planet, he wasn't that far from it.

"Six, be advised that I'm taking fire here."

"Roger. Say location."

Another blast came at him, and for the first time, Carson thought he saw the enemy. It was a large ship that was chasing him. They were using the equivalent of a battleship to hunt down a motorboat. They were expending a great amount of effort to destroy him.

Carson decided he didn't have time to waste on discussions with Savage Six. No time whatsoever. He pushed his tiny scout ship, trying to accelerate even more. He pushed it to the limit, redlining it, and then tried to get a little more speed out of it.

There were defensive weapons on the scout craft. A couple of missiles, a torpedo and his laser, but he believed that even if he hit the enemy with all of it at once, it wouldn't do much more than chip the paint. He needed to escape.

There were two choices. He could reverse his course and head for the planet, letting the atmosphere protect him. Or he could run for his own fleet, letting the larger ships inhibit the enemy. Using his small flatscreen, it seemed he had only a single choice. It had to be the planet. The fleet was too far away and the enemy was gaining too fast.

Again he yanked the yoke and the tiny ship looped around, suddenly racing back the way it had come. Carson knew it would look to the enemy on the ship as if he were attacking. He wanted to catch them off guard for a moment.

Beams burst from the side of the enemy ship, marking his location in space. Carson was aimed right at the center of it. He turned slightly and pushed down on the yoke abruptly. The enemy continued to fire, the lasers flashing out, but they didn't hit Carson.

He raced under the enemy ship, looking up at it, but could see nothing of it other than a wavering of the starlight around it that looked like heat waves rising from a sun-hot highway.

And then he was beyond it, the nose of his ship centered on the enemy's planet. At first it was basketball-sized, hanging in front of him. It grew rapidly until it filled the cockpit canopy with its glow.

Carson turned slightly away from the planet. The trick was not to hit the atmosphere at too steep an angle or one too shallow. He didn't want to burn up, and he didn't want to bounce back into space.

Glancing to the rear, he could no longer see the enemy ship.

He hoped it would take it longer to turn and that by the time it could do so, he'd have disappeared into the clutter of the planet's atmosphere.

Checking his screen, he could see nothing in front of him other than the planet. There were no batteries down there gearing up to fire at him. There were no indications that anyone on the planet knew he was coming at them.

Something flashed past him, its glowing engine marking its path. A moment later it detonated. The shock waves rocked Carson's ship but did nothing to harm it.

And then he was deep enough into the planet's atmosphere that the cloud cover hid him. He knew the enemy would have instruments that could see through the clouds like they weren't there, but now he felt safe.

"Bridge, Surveillance. We've got another four ships appearing near the gas giant off our starboard."

"Size and type?" asked Clemens.

"We have nothing on that. Their course is taking them away from us."

"Keep them in sight." Clemens touched another button. "Targeting, did you monitor?"

"Targeting, aye. We have them and are ready to fire on them. They are moving toward the extreme range."

Clemens shot a glance at the screen but there was nothing to see. To the officers in Targeting, he said, "Do not fire at them."

"Aye, Captain."

"Plot, where are they going?"

"Plot, here, Captain. We haven't had them in sight long enough to get a good plot on them."

"Keep me informed."

"Aye, sir."

Clemens studied the screen and then asked, "What the hell is the status of Knight and Negev? Put it on the screen."

"Aye, Captain."

Now he could see the two ships maneuvering. It looked as if they were dancing around one another, attacking an empty hole in space. There were flashes from the missiles and torpedoes and the stabbing of lasers and particle beams.

"Can someone give me a look at the enemy?"

"I can put in a computer simulation," said the Intelligence Officer. "Might not be completely accurate."

"Throw it up," said Clemens.

Now he could see the object of Knight's and Negev's attack. It was a single enemy ship, maybe nine hundred feet long and two or three hundred feet wide. It fired at them, but the attack was half-hearted. One or two missiles, a beam that was absorbed by the shields, and then nothing.

Both Knight and Negev suddenly reversed. Their engines glowed brightly as they accelerated and then fired missiles and torpedoes into the enemy ship.

The center of the screen began to glow. At first a dull spot that flared suddenly as the enemy ship vanished, consumed by fire.

Clemens nodded gravely. This time there wasn't a celebration on the bridge. It might have been that everyone realized it could have been one of their ships. It could have been friends who had died in the explosion.

As Clemens turned his attention away from the screen, the Intelligence Officer on the bridge said, "I think they're getting out. We should go after them."

Clemens said, "Give me a map."

"On the right screen, Captain."

"Show me the enemy ships."

"In red, Captain."

Clemens leaned forward and studied the map. As he watched the enemy ships, it became clear to him that they were leaving the system. There was no evidence they were maneuvering to attack.

"Captain, Targeting. The enemy ships have almost moved out of range."

"Hold your fire," said Clemens.

"Sir," said the Intelligence Officer, "we need to attack them before they get clear."

"No," said Clemens. "My orders were quite clear on that

point. I am to maneuver only to protect the troop ships. I am not free to engage the enemy if he is running away."

"Bridge, Surveillance. We've got something going on closer in."

"On the screen."

"Nothing to see, Captain. Just an indication of something going on. It looks like the enemy is after one of the scout craft."

"Helm, let's reverse course to zero-four-five decimal one-one-six."

"Helm, aye."

Clemens watched as the scene on the center screen changed until the planet was centered in it. There was nothing to see there. Just the openness of space and the planet looking like a small blue marble.

"Bridge, Targeting. I've got a lock on something dead ahead."

"Targeting, if it doesn't answer the IFF interrogation, you are authorized to fire."

"Targeting, aye."

"Give me an expanded picture with the troop ships in it," said Clemens.

A moment later the scene changed again. "Leopold reports all troops with his group are away, and he is retiring at high speed. There was no enemy fire encountered during the deployment."

That meant that Clemens didn't have to worry about the transports. They were free to maneuver for their own safety. The people on the ground were probably protected because a counterattack from space would do as much damage to the city as it would to the attack force.

"Bridge, Targeting. We're firing now."

Clemens didn't respond. He saw the results on the screen. Lasers, particle beams and missiles all flashed. The path of the missiles was a twisting pattern that arced toward the enemy vessel.

"He's firing at the missiles."

Two of them exploded, but the others ran unscathed. The beams played across the invisible hull of the enemy ship creating hot spots. There was a moment when it seemed the enemy was dead in space, and then suddenly the ship turned, as if to attack.

"Targeting, they're making a run on us."

"Aye, Captain. We're ready."

"You may fire at will," said Clemens.

There was a hesitation and then a spread of torpedoes appeared, running straight at the enemy. Just as the first of the enemy beams fired, the torpedoes all detonated in a blinding white flash. The shaped charges blasted radiation at the enemy ship.

The enemy ship absorbed the blast, and for a moment the hull radiated with a dull green light. On the screen, Clemens could see that the ship wasn't as large as his or some of the others they had engaged. It was a disc-shaped thing with dual fins on what he thought was the back of it.

"Enemy's getting the hell out of here, Captain," said the Intelligence Officer.

"Is he heading away from the planet and our troop ships?" asked Clemens.

"Aye, Captain. He's tailing away, dropping down and to the left. He apparently is unaware of our troop ships."

"Then let him go," said Clemens.

"Yes, sir."

"Surveillance, what is the position of the four enemy ships now?"

"They're trying to get out of the system. They are not maneuvering to attack."

Clemens fell back in his chair and said, "Main screen, give me a map, plotting the enemy's ships and their currently held courses."

"Aye, Captain."

The system appeared, the sun reduced to a pinpoint of light in one corner, the planets strung out across the screen, and the enemy's ships marked by flashing lights with their flight paths glowing behind them.

There was nothing obvious in the enemy's distribution or in the headings of the ships. It was a random pattern that suggested the enemy was getting the hell out as quickly as he could. Two or three of the enemy's ships were operating with each other, but some of them were on their own. There was no coordination to their formations.

"That everyone?" asked Clemens.

"Surveillance has put up everything they have."

"Show me our ships including the pickets and scouts," said Clemens.

"Wait one, sir. Here it comes now," said the Intelligence Officer, punching buttons in front of him.

The scene changed slightly so that several of the ships could be clustered near the top of the screen. There was no pattern there. No obvious points of enemy attack. The distribution of the Earth fleet had everything covered. The enemy couldn't attack the troops on the ground without running into several Earth ships. They could not get to the troop ships without hitting more battle craft.

"Surveillance," said Clemens.

"Surveillance, aye."

"I want a complete sweep of space around us. I want a good, solid sweep. Miss nothing."

"Aye, sir."

Clemens kept his eyes on the main flatscreen, watching as the ships changed position. There was nothing to suggest the enemy was going to attack. They had fanned out, spreading out so they were no longer in a position to protect one another. Their unit integrity was falling apart. It looked as if they were fleeing and that bothered Clemens.

"Intelligence, you have anything new from the planet's surface?"

"Negative, Captain. They're maintaining radio silence. Planetary surveillance has been limited, but from what we've seen, our people are not meeting with any resistance from the enemy."

"I don't get it," said Clemens. "It looks as if they're abandoning the system without a fight."

"Captain, we've detected another fourteen enemy ships," said the Intelligence Officer.

Clemens turned and looked over his shoulder at the man who had spoken. "And?"

"They seem to be getting the hell out too, sir. They're avoiding a fight."

"This doesn't make sense," said Clemens. But privately he hoped that it was true.

17

TORRENCE NO LONGER cared about the timetable. It was already shot to hell. Now she wanted to secure the edge of the city before moving into it. She stayed inside the building, out of the snow, wind and cold and watched as half a dozen soldiers fought their way forward toward the next building in the complex.

"Looks like the snow is slowing down," said a woman next to her.

Torrence looked at Martha Moore. She was a young NCO. "Snow shouldn't be a problem for us," said Torrence.

"No, ma'am."

The short-com crackled. "We've hit the building. It appears deserted. There are two more in front of us."

"Hold there," said Torrence. She glanced at the men and women behind her. They were all standing back, away from the outside door in the warmth of the enemy building. Water had pooled around their feet as the snow caught on their uniforms melted rapidly.

To Moore, she said, "Let's get everyone moving. Out and up to the next line."

Moore whirled and waved a hand. "You heard the Colonel. Let's get going."

They swarmed toward the door and then through it. Torrence watched them go. She stepped out after them and could now see the buildings in front of her. Moore was right; the snow was letting up.

Torrence fell in behind the rest of the troops as they struggled through the snow to the new buildings. Smoke was pouring from one of the doors. Two soldiers lay dead in the snow.

"We took it away from them. Minor resistance," said a squad leader.

"You get their weapons systems knocked out?" asked Torrence.

The man shrugged. "What weapons systems? There was nothing here that was a weapon. Large magnetic field generated in the basement area. Might have been used only to produce electric power."

Torrence nodded and for the first time keyed the long-com. "Battalion commanders, report progress."

"First battalion is down. Light resistance."

"Second battalion has met no resistance. We're having trouble reaching all objectives."

"Third battalion is down and moving."

"Fourth battalion has reached the outskirts of the city and is moving forward."

Torrence used her heads-up display. She could see the edge of the city and the locations of all the battalions. It seemed they had moved on in. They owned the edge of the city at the moment.

As she shut it off, one of the men yelled. "There's something moving out there! Coming at us!"

Torrence turned and looked. With the snow tapering to a gentle shower, she could see the mass coming at them. It was obvious that it wasn't human.

"Stand by for a counterattack," she yelled.

One man ran past her. He pointed to the right and said, "Fill in the gap there."

Two soldiers struggled to turn a machine-gun around and plug in the powerpack. Another scooped snow up, piling it in front of the weapon. It wouldn't turn a shot but it would make it difficult to see the weapon.

Half a dozen soldiers ran by. They were heading to the other side of the building. Another looked up at the low-hanging roof. "We could get the high ground."

Torrence nodded. "Put somebody up there now."

The soldiers scattered, forming a thin line. They scrambled, searching for cover, but there wasn't much. A fence and the side of the building. There were a couple of shallow depressions, partially hidden in the snow. Men and women ran to them, diving and trying to lose themselves.

"They're about a hundred yards away!" screamed a man.

"Prepare to fire," ordered Torrence.

There was a sudden burst from the right. A dozen beams slashed through the air, sizzling as they reached the enemy. There was a shout and the enemy howled. They surged forward, running at the soldiers.

"Take them. Take them, *now!*" ordered Torrence.

The whole line fired. Red and green rays danced out. The snow seemed to absorb some of them, glowing with the bright colors. There were detonations. Sudden bright orange flashes and fountains of dark brown soil. It turned into a Technicolor war, but no one had the time to appreciate that.

The enemy shot back. Blue and yellow beams. They touched soldiers and were absorbed by the wire mesh of the combat uniforms. The men and women dodged right and left, trying to get out of the beams.

Torrence crouched near the corner of a building, her weapon pointed around it. The wall above her head was hit by one of the beams. It began to glow a bright red and the stone exploded as it superheated. The flying rock knocked her down, but didn't hurt her. She rolled away from it and aimed again, but she didn't fire.

The enemy was moving in jumps. They would fire, run, dive and fire again. Around her, the soldiers were shooting. Beams flashed and disappeared. The sky around her, seeming to grow bright, was filled with them. Reds, greens, yellows and blues reflected from the snow-covered ground.

One of the men near her was hit in the face by a beam. Part of it was absorbed by the hood he wore, but part of it hit bare flesh. Skin superheated and began to bubble. The man screamed, though his hand was now up to protect his eyes, but it was too late.

Torrence fired at the enemy. She watched her beam touch the shoulder of one of them. It tried to spin away and then fell, disappearing into the snow.

Her soldiers were shouting, some of it unintelligible. They were screaming just to be screaming. Others were calling for help or trying to direct fire. Beams continued to flash. Grenades were thrown, exploding. The air was filled with the crackle of the beams, the shouts of the wounded and dying and the detonation of grenades.

As quickly as it came, the attack stopped. The enemy seemed to vanish. Torrence saw a couple of them turn to run. Others fell into the snow.

The firing around her tapered off. Just a few of the lasers and one or two of the heavier weapons. Torrence let them fire. They didn't have to worry about running out of energy.

A man ran up, saluted in violation of policy, and announced, "We have them on the run."

Torrence used the short-com. "Give me a report."

"First squad here. Enemy is cleared of the field. I think there are some wounded."

"Where'd they go?"

"Retreated toward the center of the city. Do you want us to follow?"

"Negative," said Torrence. "We'll move slowly on this. Who's got the point?"

Ramey's voice interrupted. "Byner should have it with his squad."

"Byner," said Torrence.

"Byner here. Go."

"Give me a short count."

"Roger."

While Byner did that, Torrence keyed the heads-up and spotted Byner's position on it. She could see that the enemy attack had passed right by them.

"Do you have any enemy in sight?"

"That's a negative. They retreated from here, moving toward the middle of the city."

"Can you follow them?"

"Roger. That's no problem. They left a wide trail in the snow."

"Do so," said Torrence. "But stay in touch. Do not get out of range of the short-com."

"Roger."

"Ramey," Torrence said, "check the enemy. I don't want to find half of them are playing dead out there."

"Roger."

A moment passed and then men and women began moving out over the field. She watched as they moved from body to body, checking each one.

Torrence stepped to the right where Martha Moore lay. It was obvious that she was dead. An enemy beam had hit her in the eyes and fried her brain. Smoke was drifting from a hole in Moore's head.

Torrence moved forward then, into a sheltered courtyard bordered by the enemy's buildings. She stood there looking at them, surprised at how much they looked like the buildings of Earth. She'd thought that the enemy, since they were aliens, would build structures quite different from those on Earth. But then many Earth structures were designed for function rather than aesthetics. There simply weren't that many ways to construct a building.

"Colonel, we're ready to go."

She looked at the woman. "You get a count on the casualties on our side?"

"No ma'am, but they were light. A couple of dead. That's all. We got them marked."

"Good. Let's go."

Carson was surprised by the buffeting when he hit the planet's atmosphere. It was as if he were in a glider and had flown into a thunderstorm. He was thrown around, the scout ship shaking and bouncing. The flatscreen flared brightly, popped and went out.

"Shit!" yelled Carson, thinking of the words he'd spoken to the teenaged technician. There was nothing that Carson could do to regain his flatscreen.

He punched a button and the canopy cleared, but that did him no good. He had a fine view of the sky above him, and if he rolled right or left, he would be able to see the ground. In level flight, he couldn't see anything below him.

The buffeting stopped for a moment and Carson started to relax. Smoke was curling from around the corner of the flatscreen and he knew he had an electrical fire.

"Shit!" he yelled again. He hit a button to activate a fire extinguisher, knowing that it would knock out more of his electronics.

There was a loud bang behind him and the ship began to plummet. Carson pulled on the yoke and the nose of the ship rose slightly but the buffeting was back. His ship was no longer a glider. It had been turned into a lifting body. He could control the descent but there would be no maneuvering it. And without the flatscreen, he couldn't see what was below him. He couldn't plan the approach.

Taking one hand from the yoke, he jerked the belts of his harness tighter. He glanced to the right, but could see nothing other than the clouds. He was caught in the middle of the planet's atmosphere without a clue as to where he was. He could be heading for mountains or an ocean or anything.

He looked at the altimeter. The electronic one was out and the pressure one was geared for Earth normal. He didn't know if it was accurate or not, but suspected it was useless.

Taking a chance, Carson rolled to the right slightly so that he could look down. The speed of the descent increased. And Carson couldn't see anything for the moment. Just more of the clouds looking as if he'd been caught in a wad of dirty white cotton.

Then through a break he could see the surface of the planet ten, twelve thousand feet below him. There was a single, large open plain. It looked as if he'd be able to land on it. Just as suddenly as it had opened, the hole closed, and Carson was again wrapped in the overcast.

"Only one thing to do," Carson announced to himself. He rolled back to the left and leveled off. He aimed in the general direction of the open plain, hoping for the best there.

The pressure altimeter was continuing to unwind rapidly, and it suggested that he was twenty thousand feet above the planet. Carson was sure he was closer than that.

And then he punched through the bottom of the cloud deck. He could see the plain spread out in front of him. Carson tried to level the craft, bringing the nose down so that he could get a good look at the open plain. That caused him to pick up speed rapidly.

Carson pulled on the yoke, and the nose came back up. Now he focused his attention on the horizon in front of him. The light snow was making it difficult to see it. Carson would have to rely on his instruments to keep his ship level.

Carson fought the controls. The nose wanted to fall, but Carson held it up, trying to reduce his forward speed as much as he could. He needed to slow the descent.

The problem was that he could not see the real horizon. It was lost in the snow. There was a line of front of him that could have been it, but he couldn't tell.

Then suddenly he hit the ground with a bone-jarring smack. The ship bounced high, wallowed like a huge, overweight bird and fell back into the snow with a splash.

The ship skidded, but there was nothing Carson could do to stop the slide. He fought to keep the ship straight, watching as the snow washed over the canopy like the surf on a beach. There was a grinding under the ship as rocks, logs and dirt sliced at it.

The ship dropped suddenly as if it had just fallen off the edge of a short cliff. It bounced again and then slammed into the hill in front of him. Carson was thrown forward, but the restraining straps of the seatbelt held him fast, cutting into his shoulders and belly.

But he was stopped. He was down on the planet's surface. He took a deep breath and then coughed. The cockpit was filling with smoke. Something was on fire.

Carson reached down and punched a button. There were four

quiet pops as the explosive bolts that held the canopy in place fired. An instant later, there was another, and the canopy was ejected. Cold air swirled in, clearing out the smoke in seconds.

Unbuckling himself and then standing up, Carson said, "Guess I better go find the infantry."

Richard Peel walked along the line his troops had created. Their mission was to act as a blocking force which meant they were to find a position on the eastern side of the city, fill in and then wait for the enemy to appear.

He came to a soldier who had scooped the snow out of a shallow depression and was now lying in it. She was stretched out, her rifle in the snow next to her. Peel stopped behind the woman, waited for a moment and then kicked the bottom of her foot.

She rolled to the right and said, "What the hell you doing?" Then she saw who it was and added, "Sir."

"No," said Peel, "don't get up. Just lay there and explain why your weapon is in the snow."

"Snow won't hurt it," she said.

Peel crouched down and grabbed a handful of snow. He squeezed it tightly, but it was a dry snow and didn't pack well. He let it fall and then said, "When I was in basic training, we were taught to respect our weapons. We were taught that the weapon came first because if our weapons failed, then we died. We did not set our weapon in the snow even if the snow wouldn't hurt it."

"Yes, sir," she said, but she made no move toward her weapon.

Peel looked at her for a moment and then roared, "Pick the fucking weapon up and clean it off. Do not put it down again until we're back on the ship."

"Yes, sir."

Peel stood up and looked to the right. "Where's your squad leader?"

"Over there, sir. By the tree."

Peel shook his head in disgust. He walked over and said, "When we return to the ship, this whole squad will pull every extra duty detail that comes along for the next month. That means everyone, squad leader included."

"Yes, sir," said the squad leader. "May I ask why?"

"Why?" snorted Peel. "Make that two months. And if you still want to know, you can ask the members of your squad. Maybe one of them knows the reason."

With that Peel spun and continued his survey of the line. He found another soldier whose weapon had collected some snow, jumped on him and then moved down to the building they had taken over for headquarters. Peel kicked his right foot against the doorjamb, stepped through and repeated the process, knocking the snow from his left boot.

Inside, he moved rapidly across the room, opened the door and entered the next. The warmth wrapped around him like a blanket on a winter's evening. He stood for a moment, letting his body warm up and then moved toward the far wall where the RTO had set up the radio equipment that included the up-link to the ships.

"Everything's set," said the NCO, grinning. "If we end radio silence, I'll be able to contact the ship."

"You heard anything?"

"Colonel Torrence used the long-com to contact her battalions. They're behind schedule but report that resistance is light."

"Fucking Torrence," said Peel. "The General seems to think she can walk on water."

"She was his exec when he was a regimental commander," said the NCO.

"I don't believe I asked for an analysis from you," said Peel coldly.

"Yes, sir. Sorry."

"There a response from the general since she broke the radio silence?"

"No, sir. And it wasn't much of a break. She just asked for the battalion commanders to report and then went right off the air."

Peel nodded and turned away. He walked over to where the regimental intell officer had set up. He'd set a flatscreen against the wall, had the powerpack set up under it and had keyed in some of the data.

"What you got for me?" asked Peel.

"Not much. I've tried to plot Torrence's regiment, but the information was incomplete. And Jefferson, along with his platoon, have deployed around here."

"How good are your guesses, Captain?"

The officer shrugged. "I'm afraid they're not very good. I did the best with the information I had, but with the snow and the lack of up-link to the fleet, I'm shooting in the dark."

Peel pulled the hood of his uniform off and ran a hand through his hair. "I want you to get up-to-date information for me."

"Yes, sir."

Peel stood and studied the map. The city was oval-shaped with the southern end more pointed than the northern. The red areas on the western side, southern end and the eastern side marked the locations of Jefferson's regiments. Along the northern side was a river that made retreat by the enemy a little more difficult.

"What's that in the middle of the city?" asked Peel.

"Some kind of power-plant I would imagine. Could be a large housing complex. I don't know."

"Your job is to know these things. I don't want to hear about your speculations."

"Yes, sir. Intelligence about that was sketchy. They didn't survey as well as they could have because they didn't want to tip their hand."

"Captain, you're giving me excuses for your failure to have answers. I'm not interested in that."

"Yes, sir."

"Now," said Peel, "what would happen if that power center was suddenly knocked out?"

"I imagine it would disrupt the enemy's ability to retaliate."

"So if we were to detach a company or two with orders to take it out, then that might end this little engagement, and we could all go back to the fleet."

"I'm sure that General Jefferson was aware of that," said the

Intelligence Officer. "There must have been a reason he didn't target it."

"I believe that Colonel Torrence was given it as a target, and she's failed to take it. I think I'll do it for her."

"Yes, sir."

Peel stared at the flatscreen for a moment and then nodded. "I believe that's exactly what I'll do."

18

WITH THE PLATOON spread out near him, Jefferson worked his way around the outskirts of the city, searching for Torrence and her regiment. They passed one battalion as it moved into the city, hopping from building to building, clearing them as they searched for the enemy.

Jefferson used the short-com to coordinate with the units they passed, letting them know he and the platoon were coming up and then slipping behind them. He saw some of the soldiers either standing guard or moving among the various structures.

After nearly an hour, they rounded one building and found the remains of a skirmish. There were bodies scattered in the snow, craters marking the explosions of grenades and scorch marks from the lasers.

They moved over the field slowly, checking the bodies to make sure there would be no surprises. They followed the tracks, searching.

Over the short-com, Jefferson said, "Apache Six, this is Kiowa Six."

"Go," said a voice he recognized as Torrence.

"Check your heads-up. We're coming up behind you."

"Roger. Got you. You're about two hundred yards behind us now."

CHAIN OF COMMAND

"Roger that."

Arney, without being told, ordered the platoon to fan out and then began moving toward Torrence's forward position. Jefferson followed along, searching the ground around them, looking for signs that the enemy was sneaking back to infiltrate behind Torrence.

They came up behind Torrence's position and halted. Jefferson now used the short-com. "Apache Six, we're right behind you now."

"Roger. I have you on the heads-up. Come ahead."

Jefferson stood up and began to walk toward Torrence's position. Through the snow, he could see her and two of her officers standing near the doorway of a building.

Torrence grinned as he approached. "Nice of you to join us, General."

Jefferson brushed the snow from his face and said, "This is the worst weather I've seen in a long time."

"Kind of explains why we're running behind schedule."

Jefferson nodded and then asked, "Resistance has been light?"

"More than light," said Torrence. "It's nearly nonexistent. I don't begin to understand it." She pointed at the ground. "Enemy in fairly small numbers has been moving in that direction. We're following."

"How far behind are you?"

"Half-mile. Maybe less." She glanced to the rear and then said, "I've got to tell you, we haven't found much in the way of defensive positions. A few of the objectives have been taken, but they weren't the weapons systems we expected to find."

Jefferson stared at the ground. "I don't begin to understand it either."

"We've seen indications that there is some kind of concentration in the center of the city, but we've been careful to avoid it for the moment."

"Any ideas what it is?"

Torrence shrugged. "How can we tell? We're dealing with an alien mind here, and we don't know that much about them.

Maybe when it snows, they all get together to wait out the storm. People sometimes hold hurricane parties."

"Snowstorm is a lot tamer than a hurricane."

"Maybe they're allergic to snow. Hell, General, I don't know. All I can tell you is that resistance to the landing has been light, and we can't pinpoint any concentrations of enemy soldiers."

"What's the overall status of your regiment?" asked Jefferson.

"We're moving slowly forward. I don't want anyone to surge too far out in front and get cut off."

"I think it's time to make a real move," said Jefferson. "I've got the whole brigade down now. We can take a couple of chances."

"Yes, sir," said Torrence. She reached up and touched the side of her head to push the earpiece of the short-com deeper. "Cheyenne Six, this is Apache Six."

"Go."

"I want you to move out now. You'll be spearheading. Your target is the main structure at coordinates eight-one-five-two-seven-seven."

"Understood. Jump off in five minutes."

"Negative," Torrence said. "You go now."

"Roger. We're moving now."

She turned to Jefferson. "You sure this is a good idea?"

"Hell," said Jefferson, "I don't know. But I think getting the prisoners freed will get us the hell out of here faster than anything."

"Then we've got to do it."

Ramey watched as two of the other companies moved from the protection of the buildings, filed into the streets and began moving forward. The streets were wide, but with the thick blanket of snow, it was impossible to tell how they were surfaced. All he knew was that there were wide areas between buildings and those wide areas looked to be streets.

The snow was falling gently now and the wind had died away. He could see an orange glow of light in the distance but no sign of anything living near that glow. There were no tracks on the street, making it look as if the city were deserted.

Sticking close to the side of the building, his back to the smooth wall, he slipped along. He could easily see the squad that was moving on the street opposite him and the rest of the company spread out behind him.

Crowley was leading two of the platoons up another side-street, and they were in communication with one another over the short-com. No one had said a word, and no one had fired a shot since they had begun the move. The only sound was Crowley's quiet breathing being transmitted by the open mike of her short-com. Ramey said nothing because he found the sound comforting.

They reached a corner and Ramey halted momentarily. He poked his head out, glanced right and left and then waved a hand at the sergeant following him. Without a sound, the woman sprinted forward around Ramey and out into the intersection. She leaped several times, hurdling snow drifts, and ran for the edge of the building. She reached it, dived for cover and then climbed to her feet. There was no evidence the enemy was waiting for her.

Over the short-com, Ramey said, "Crossing the street now."

Crowley answered with, "Roger. We'll be doing the same in sixty seconds."

Ramey ducked his head and then jumped out. He ran through the snow, following the path made by his NCO, knowing that he should be cutting a new one.

Around him a dozen others were running, crossing the street and diving for cover. Ramey hit the side of the building, glanced back down the cross-street but could see nothing other than empty ground covered in snow.

He watched as the rest of the company followed him and then was on the short-com. "We're moving up."

"Roger. We're a little behind."

Ramey nodded, knowing that she wouldn't be able to see it. He hesitated, giving her a chance to catch up and then waved his point man forward.

At first they had been checking each of the buildings, looking for signs of the enemy, but they failed to find anything.

The enemy had slipped away. It seemed the city was deserted.

Crowley came on the short-com. "We've got an open door here. We're checking."

There was a sudden blast, a single flat bang. Ramey instinctively dropped to one knee. Over the short-com, he asked, "What was that?"

"Grenade. One of ours. Should have warned you."

"Yeah," said Ramey to himself.

They rushed along that street until they came to another cross-street, but this time Ramey didn't send out his point. He could now see the huge building that marked the city center. It was a dull gray structure with only a few lights behind the windows.

"We've reached the end of the line," said Ramey on the short-com.

"We're about thirty seconds out," responded Crowley.

The NCO who had been on the point slipped back and crouched with a knee in the snow. "Doesn't look like anyone's home in there."

Ramey flipped his image enhancer down and swept the front of the building. Only a few of the windows had light showing in them, and there was nothing going on inside.

Using the long-com, he said, "Apache Six, we have reached the target. There is nothing happening here."

"Roger. Deploy and wait."

"Roger." Ramey glanced down at the NCO and said, "Get the people spread out. If you can find a place to warm up a little, rotate the people in and out. No more than ten pencent in there at any one time."

"Yes, sir."

As the NCO ran off, Ramey turned to study the front of the building. It was one hell of a way to fight a war.

Cooper heard some of the messages on the short-com and picked up the orders issued on the long-com. But he didn't want to move. With the remains of his squad scattered around him dead, he didn't think anyone would notice his absence. Besides, his shoulder still throbbed.

Franz, however, had other ideas. She listened to the orders

and then pointed through the falling snow. "That direction," she said. "That's the center of the city."

"We don't have to go," said Cooper.

"Staying here won't do us much good," said Franz. "Alone, we're vulnerable."

"We get into the fight," said Cooper, "it's going to be worse for us."

"Come on," said Franz. "On your feet. We've got to catch the rest of the regiment."

"I'm hurt," said Cooper. "My shoulder's killing me and I can't move my arm."

"You're not hurt that badly," said Franz. "You want to stay here and freeze, or you want to find someplace warm where we can hide?"

"You're not really going to look for a place to hide," said Cooper.

Franz shrugged. "No, I guess not. But we can't sit around back here either. We've got to catch the rest of the company and join them."

Cooper nodded, climbed to his feet and brushed the snow from his uniform. He checked his rifle and saw there was nothing that would clog it or bend the laser beam around and nothing that would interfere with the operation of it.

Staring into the distance, Cooper asked, "Why not just fall back?"

"Because soldiers go forward," said Franz. "You going to follow me?"

"Sure, Sarge. Anything you say."

Franz began walking toward the center of the city. She veered to the right and moved along the wall of a long, low building. She kept glancing back to make sure that Cooper was with her.

"Don't worry, Sarge, I'll stick with you."

They moved beyond the building and entered the city proper. The one thing Cooper noticed was the silence. He was part of an invading army moving in on an enemy city, and there was nothing to hear but the falling of the snow. It created a blanket of quiet that absorbed the sounds.

They followed a street that had not been used for hours.

They reached an intersection and Franz stopped. She pointed at the tracks and said, "Looks like our people are moving in that direction."

"So we follow them," said Cooper.

"But carefully. We don't want them opening fire on us," said Franz.

Before Franz could move again, Cooper asked, "Sarge, are you sure this is a good idea? Maybe we should hang back and form an impromptu rear guard." He held onto his shoulder, massaging it gently.

"The war is in front of us," said Franz. "That's where we should be." She carefully avoided looking at him because she didn't want to be reminded of his injury.

"Sure, but there's no reason for us to rush into a battle. It'll be there when we get there."

Franz fell back against the side of a building and then crouched. She wiped a hand across her face and said, "I want to get with another platoon. I don't like this feeling of it all hanging out. The enemy finds us and we're going to be in a world of hurt."

"Enemy's all in front of us," said Cooper. "There are soldiers between them and us. We can catch some rest here. We're safe here."

Franz looked at him and said, "Maybe it wouldn't hurt to take it easy. As long as we get into the fight before it's over."

"My plan exactly."

19

PEEL DIDN'T LIKE leading the regiment into battle. He believed the commander's place was in the rear, directing the troops as they assaulted their objectives. He'd spent his time as a platoon leader and a company commander, so he'd been in the lead on the attack. Of course, he tended to forget that those assaults were part of training exercises where people were only simulated-killed for the duration of the exercise. He'd never led real troops into a real battle.

But now he was out in front of the troops, working his way along one of the snow-choked streets. He kept moving, punching through the drifts piled up next to the buildings, following the path created by the point.

They met no resistance and didn't see any enemy soldiers, alive or dead. The streets were as deserted as the Mayan ruins on Earth.

That made things easier on Peel. He had decided that no resistance meant no enemy soldiers around him. He felt comfortable ignoring the objectives he had been given during the briefings. If there were no soldiers to man the suspected defensive positions, there was no reason to attack them. Therefore, he could make good time pressing for the center of the city and the citadel marking the overall objective of the entire brigade.

"Colonel," said one of the NCOs coming back to join him. "The point has reached the center of the city. The citadel is right in front of us."

Peel nodded and stepped around the soldier. Keeping his back to the wall, he moved forward until he could see the citadel rising from the center of the city like some kind of bizarre fortress.

Someone came up beside Peel and crouched. He leaned close and said, "Looks like it'll be easy to breach. Doesn't look to be fortified."

Peel glanced to the right and saw one of his young officers. She had joined the regiment about six months earlier, had stayed out of his way and Peel had no idea what her name was.

"You can never tell," he said. He used the short-com. "Davis, you want to come up here?"

"Yes, sir."

He started to ask each of his battalion commanders to report, but knew he'd have to switch to the long-com. He didn't want Jefferson or Torrence to know what he was planning.

When Davis arrived, he said, "Looks like the place is basically deserted. I want to be ready to move against it in about twenty minutes. First and second battalions to assault with the rest of the regiment held in reserve. I'll want two companies from the fourth scattered behind us to form a rear guard just in case. We'll need to pass the word with runners and on the short-com."

"Yes, sir. But shouldn't we wait for the rest of the brigade?"

"No," said Peel. "This is our baby. We're here and in position. We can take it now and save everyone a lot of aggravation."

"Yes, sir."

Davis retreated, keeping his head down. He pushed back to where a company commander was crouched and began to give him instructions.

Peel crouched next to the wall of the building and looked across the street at the citadel. He was reminded of pictures of the Pentagon he'd seen. There was a vast area around it that could have been a parking lot if the enemy still used individual ground vehicles for transportation. There were some trees, looking lonely in the open areas. There were mounds of snow that might have marked fence lines or maybe it was snow scraped from the parking lots. There was almost no cover from that area to the side of the building. But then there didn't seem to be firing ports, shutters or reinforced walls. Just a normal building sitting in the center of the city like some kind of giant shopping mall.

If they'd been on Earth facing humans, Peel would have sent out scouts dressed in civilian clothes to recon the area. Here there was nothing he could do except study the building and the ground around it with the image enhancer on his helmet, search for infrared clues that the enemy was waiting and try to spot the gun emplacements so he could deal with them as the regiment moved.

Davis returned and knelt next to him. His breath was rasping in his throat; it created little puffs of smoke. "We're about ready. Word is being passed."

"Let's move now," said Peel. "First company out of the streets and over to that fence."

"Yes, sir." Davis used his short-com and gave the order. He finished with, "Move it *now!*"

Peel saw the first of his soldiers run from cover. Small, dark shapes sprinting through the snow until they reached the fence. They spread out along it.

Peel saw there was no firing from the citadel. There was no indication anyone in it had seen his men and women. Satisfied that it was safe, Peel stood and then bent at the waist like a man in a strong wind; he ran forward. Reaching the fence, he threw himself to the ground, splashing the snow away from him. He pointed his rifle up at one of the lighted windows but didn't fire.

Glancing to the right, he saw a surging line of soldiers filtering out of the ends of the streets, running toward the fence. They crouched there, some of them aiming up at the building while others sat, their backs to the snow and their heads down.

"Company A is in position," said the commander using the short-com.

Peel keyed his and said, "B company, are you ready to move yet?"

"Company B is in position."

"Wait one," said Peel. He turned and looked over the top of the snow at the building. Still nothing. "Company A, let's take it to the wall. Company B, as A moves, fall into position behind them. Company C, move up to B's position."

"A, roger."

"B, roger."

"C, roger."

Now the first soldiers were scrambling from their protection. One of them slipped and fell face down in the snow but was up and running a moment later. As the last of them climbed over the snow barricade, the soldiers of B company ran from the protection of the streets.

Peel waited, but still there was no firing. As the men and women reached the halfway point, he climbed over the snow and slid down to the ground. He glanced back and saw some of Company B running out.

Then he got to his feet and began to lope across the open ground. He watched as the first of the soldiers reached the wall. They spread out, covering the few doors they could locate. Once they were set, they waited for instructions.

With Jefferson right behind her, Torrence ran down the street following the path cut in the snow by those who'd gone before. They reached a cross-street but didn't hesitate. There were guards on both sides of it protecting the troops as they moved forward.

Within minutes they reached the rear of Ramey's point company and then crouched to wait as the rest of the regiment caught up. Torrence, with one shoulder against the wall, pointed at the building in front of them.

"Doesn't look much like a fort," she said. "Or much of a prison."

Jefferson knelt next to her, a hand up to shield his eyes from the snow that continued to fall. "Could be filled with the enemy just waiting for us."

"Sure."

Jefferson switched to his long-com. "Pawnee Six, report status."

There was a moment's hesitation and then Peel said, "I am in position."

"Roger. Sioux Six, say status."

"I am awaiting your instructions."

"Roger." Jefferson grinned and looked up at Torrence. "Blocking forces and reinforcements are all in position—waiting for you."

Torrence had been using her own radio. She nodded and said, "I've got one battalion running a little behind. They hit some resistance that slowed them momentarily. They're on the move now."

Jefferson checked the time. They were behind the projected timetable established before they had landed, but it didn't seem to matter. Resistance was light or completely nonexistent, and there didn't seem to be the wide range of weapons that intelligence had told them about. Almost every building they had assaulted because it had been identified as a defensive structure had turned out to house no weapons at all.

Jefferson said, "Let's get them moving. I want to report to division that we've got the city secured and the prisoners freed in the next hour or so."

"Roger that."

Jefferson stood and withdrew slightly. He backed up until he was against the smooth material that formed the wall of the building. It seemed to be slightly warm, though the snow around it was not melting.

Jefferson watched the citadel for a moment, searching for signs the enemy was still there. Or signs that the enemy had ever been there. He saw nothing other than a few lighted windows without movement behind them. It began to look as if all the intelligence had been wrong. A general bombing of the planet would have worked because there was no one around to worry about. Just a few of the enemy who were fighting a rear guard action as everyone else escaped.

* * *

"There are another twelve ships coming up, Captain," said the Intelligence Officer.

"On the screen."

"Aye, sir."

Clemens watched as the new ships climbed through the planet's atmosphere and then turned away from his ship. They ran, accelerating after the ships that had already taken off and were already fleeing.

"They're moving toward light speed," said the Intelligence Officer.

"Surveillance," said Clemens, "what can you tell me about those ships?"

"They don't appear to be warships, Captain. Configuration is wrong and we've been able to detect them easily. No attempt to hide them with stealth capabilities. Seems that they're transports of some kind."

"What in the hell is going on here?" asked Clemens.

Before anyone could answer, there was another call. "Bridge, this is Plot."

"Go."

"Projected lines based on the enemy's probable rendezvous does not, I repeat, does not, suggest they are massing for an attack."

"On the screen," said Clemens.

The images faded and then the enemy's ships appeared, looking larger than they were. All showed signs of rapid acceleration out of the system. It was like looking at the glowing exhaust pipes of jet fighters as they decided they'd had enough of the furball and it was time to break off the engagement. The dogfight had ended.

Two of the ships faded from the screen, and for an instant Clemens thought they had blown up. But there was no glowing cloud of expanding debris. Those ships had reached light speed and were no longer visible.

"Bridge, Surveillance. We're beginning to lose track of the enemy."

"Roger. Communications, get me Captains Fogel, Madison and Terrence."

"Communications ready."

"Fogel, take command of the small task group and deploy on the farside of the planet's surface. You are to survey space there, looking for a return of the enemy. You will engage any enemy ship that appears in your sector, and you will report to me on the quarter hour."

"Aye, sir."

Clemens leaned back in his chair and said, "Give a clean screen and then space forward of our position. I want to see everything."

"Aye, Captain."

Clemens watched as the screen returned to what it had been before the enemy ships had lifted from the planet. At the far edge of the screen he could see the last of the enemy ships running from the fight. They'd made no attempt to hold the system or the planet. They'd given it up too easily and that worried him greatly.

"Surveillance," said Clemens, "what do you have under observation?"

"We have four enemy ships accelerating toward light speed, all of them attempting to avoid contact with us. We have swept the outer planets and find no devices, no outposts and no concentration of enemy forces. We have detected no new concentrations of enemy ships. Everything that has been spotted has attempted to get clear of the system. They have given the system to us."

"Anything on the main planet?"

"Aye, sir. We're still getting electromagnetic, infrared and atomic radiation readings. There is a concentration of life readings nearing the center of the industrial complex."

"That's our people."

"No, sir. Readings are much too high for it to be only our people unless an additional force has been landed."

"What the hell is going on here?" Clemens asked.

"They're getting out," said the Intelligence Officer. "I think we've won."

20

WAITING WAS GOING to do no good. If the enemy was inside the citadel, then waiting just gave him time to prepare a better defense. And if he wasn't there, then waiting caused unnecessary anxiety.

Peel watched as the men and women of his command spread out to form a line that would assault the citadel. He stayed away from the doors and windows but when everyone was in position, yelled, "Let's take them!"

Two soldiers ran forward, slapped plastic explosive on one of the doors and darted away. An instant later there was a quiet hissing, then a pop and the door fell in. The two soldiers ran forward again, hit the wall hard with their backs and threw grenades in.

And the grenades came sailing right back out. Both soldiers dived away as the grenades detonated. There was a mushrooming of snow and dark brown dirt.

As soon as the grenades exploded, there was a scream from inside. The enemy rushed from the building firing lasers at the humans. Their blue and yellow beams slashed through the night, smashing into the surprised soldiers.

Peel, seeing what was happening, dived to the ground and

rolled close to the side of the building. He scooped at the snow, piling it up on himself as he tried to hide from the enemy.

One soldier stood his ground, firing at the enemy soldiers. He took several beams in the chest, but the mesh absorbed the energy. He held down the trigger of his own weapon, spraying the enemy like a firefighter with a hose.

A half-dozen of the enemy ran at him. He cut three of them down, slicing the leg off one of them, an arm from another and a huge chunk out of the side of the third. But the remaining three reached him. They jumped and bowled him over. They rolled through the snow. The soldier punched one in the face. It howled in sudden pain.

One of the beings tried to hit the soldier with its hand, but the long thin fingers with brittle bones were not made for striking. The hand shattered and the creature wailed in sudden pain. The soldier kicked the last in the chest, knocking it back and then down into the snow.

He struggled to sit up and was hit in the head by an enemy beam. He slipped back, falling into the snow and didn't move. The powerpack on his belt began to whine.

A hundred or more enemy soldiers poured from the door. They fired right and left as they ran across the open ground. They screamed at the tops of their voices. It didn't seem to be a coordinated attack.

Peel glanced up and saw one of the enemy soldiers running along the wall, heading right for him. Peel rolled to his left and aimed his rifle. He fired once and saw the beam stab out, punching into the shoulder of the enemy soldier. It spun and fell and didn't move.

Now Peel scrambled to his feet and leaned back against the wall. He fired again, but the shot was wild, missing the enemy soldiers as they ran for the fence line.

Then suddenly above them in the windows that had been darkened and along the roofline that was four stories above them, the enemy began to fire. Not the small, individual weapons, but larger lasers that punched through the mesh of the suits, baking the guts of the soldiers. Powerpacks suddenly overloaded, began to explode, the detonations sporadic at first, but then coming faster as more enemy weapons opened fire.

The attack across the open ground that looked as if it had been doomed was suddenly close to the fence line. As soldiers stood to meet the enemy, they were cut down by the high-powered weapons.

The assault reached the fence line, and the enemy struggled to climb the snowbanks. As the two sides became mixed, the firing from the citadel was directed at the soldiers still in the streets. More weapons fired, the beams crisscrossing overhead creating a net of electricity.

Soldiers fell as their uniforms failed to absorb all the energy from the enemy. Others died as their powerpacks exploded, killing them and those around them.

Peel, sitting in the snow near the base of the wall, forced himself back with the heels of his boots. He sat with his back against the wall, his rifle across his knees. His head was bowed, as if he were asleep or dead. His eyes were open and moving as he tried to watch the battle without letting the enemy know he was still alive.

The short-com crackled in his ear as the officers tried to coordinate the defense. They were asking for help, directing the fields of fire and trying to locate him, but Peel was afraid he would tell the enemy he was still alive if he used the radio.

He heard Earl, one of his company commanders, say, "First platoon is down to forty percent effectives."

"Moving up on the right of them."

"Hold short," said Earl. "Let's get some of these heavy weapons taken out."

Peel turned his head slightly. He could see the beams flashing out from the top of the building. They were raking the regiment's position across the street, tearing it apart. Peel knew there was nothing he could do.

Over the long-com, he heard, "Pawnee Six, Pawnee Six, this is Five. Say location."

Peel wasn't going to answer that either. Let his exec take command for the moment. Once the heat was off, he could get out of there and take over.

"All battalions, be advised that we've lost contact with six. I am assuming command."

CHAIN OF COMMAND

"Roger," said one of the battalion commanders. Peel didn't know who it was.

He glanced up and saw that the fight at the fence had nearly ended. His people were scattered around in the snow like so many toy soldiers dumped on the carpet. A few of them moved, but as they did, a dozen lasers punched into them.

More of the enemy was pouring from the building now. They didn't bother with the soldiers lying there. They ran across the open ground heading straight for the fence line. They fired from the hip, letting the beams rake the soldiers.

The defense at the fence line broke down suddenly. The firing there tapered off as the last of the soldiers were either killed or abandoned their positions. The fighting shifted from there to the street where the rest of the regiment waited.

Jefferson, still waiting for Torrence to get ready to move, heard the shouting on the other side of the citadel. The strobing of the colored lights reflected from the falling snow and the low-hanging clouds.

"That what I think it is?" asked Torrence.

"From the location, it looks like Peel has triggered something."

"What are we going to do?"

Jefferson shrugged. "He doesn't answer the long-com. Atmospheric conditions are playing hell with the radios. I suspect he's attacking."

"Then I'd better move to support him," said Torrence. "Divide their attention."

"I don't like rushing into this blind," said Jefferson. "They could have one hell of a defending force in there."

"So, what are we going to do?"

"There isn't much choice in the matter. Not with prisoners being held there. If you're ready, we'll have to attack. I'll have Nesmith hold her regiment in reserve right where it is now."

"Jump off in five minutes. I've already got some people moving toward the building now."

"I'll be right behind you."

"Yes, sir."

"Vicki," said Jefferson. "Good luck."

"Thanks."

As Torrence ran off, Jefferson tried the long-com again. Peel still didn't answer, but Nesmith did. Jefferson told her, "Hold where you are. Dig in and wait. Send one company on a recon toward Pawnee Six and report what's happening there."

"Roger."

Jefferson turned and saw Lieutenant Arney. "We'll be moving in support of Colonel Torrence."

"Yes, sir. We're ready."

Torrence had her regiment moving already. The men and women were filtering out of the streets, running across the open ground. They spread out, hitting all along the wall of the building but staying away from the doors. They surrounded the windows.

Jefferson, with his recon platoon, moved with them finally. They followed the regiment, dodging right and left. As he ran, Jefferson was sure he could feel an enemy rifle aimed right at him. He was sure that at any moment a beam would flash and strike him.

But then he was in the shadow of the building, where it would be nearly impossible for anyone inside to fire at him without leaning out a window or over a ledge of the roof to shoot down.

The soldiers didn't wait for more orders. They worked frantically to open up the citadel. They slapped plastic explosive on the windows, the doors and their frames. Ducking down, they prepared to blow them open. Along the line, men and women yelled, "Fire in the hole!" That was followed by dull explosions.

As the windows were blown out, the soldiers boosted one another up and into the building. A dozen, then two dozen vanished from sight.

Jefferson kept the short-com on the guard frequency. He'd be able to hear any messages broadcast, but there was nothing to hear as the soldiers infiltrated.

Torrence appeared and said, "We've taken out a door. Want to follow me?"

"I'm right behind you."

Torrence turned and ran back the way she'd come. Jefferson

followed and slipped to a stop near an entrance to the citadel. The doorway was blackened and debris littered the ground around it. A dozen soldiers had it covered.

"Anyone inside yet?"

"Yes, ma'am. Squad went through."

Torrence glanced at Jefferson, who said, "I'm right behind you."

"Come on," said Torrence, waving a hand.

They all rushed through the door and found themselves in a long and narrow room. There were doors opposite them, one of which had been blown open. Light blazed through it.

Torrence ran across the concrete floor, hit the wall next to the door and glanced in. A moment later she disappeared through it.

Jefferson followed her, running through the door and then sliding to a halt immediately. He hadn't been prepared for what he saw. The entire center of the citadel was open from below ground level to the roof four or five stories above. A wire and steel sculpture climbed toward the roof and was hung with colored lights. There were balconies around the perimeter, and there were doors beyond that. It looked like some of the fanciest hotels that had been built on Earth.

"Good God," said Jefferson.

Soldiers were running along the ground balcony, trying to secure the area. They were fanning out, checking the doors and the rooms behind them. There was shouting as orders were given, but no one was firing.

Jefferson joined in, running along the balcony, the headquarters platoon commanded by Arney right behind them. He glanced into some of the open doors as they ran by. There was overturned furniture in some of the rooms. Doors had been kicked in and debris littered the floor. There was no sign of life in any of the rooms.

They continued on and came to a narrow hallway that looked like a tunnel connecting two major parts of the citadel. There were already other soldiers there who had taken up defensive positions near it.

"What's going on here?" asked Jefferson.

"We're securing this," said an NCO without looking back at Jefferson.

"Anyone entered it?"

"Nope and I don't think any of us will. Too easy to get killed down there."

"Lieutenant," said Jefferson.

"Yes, sir," said Arney. "First squad's on me. Fourth, you're the rear guard. Let's go."

Arney dashed forward and began a sprint down the hallway. He didn't slow, but leaped over something that was hidden in the dim glow of the hallway. The members of the first squad were right behind him.

Jefferson entered the mouth of the tunnel and crouched near the wall. He flipped on the image enhancer and studied the tunnel. The walls were dark material. There were a few access doors on the right and left sides and what looked like a hatch in the ceiling about halfway down. There were no access doors on the floor which was soft, almost like astroturf or a wrestling mat. The floor, like the walls and the ceiling, was made of a dark colored material.

"Second squad," said Jefferson. "You come with me." He stood up and began walking down the tunnel, his shoulder against the left side of it. He held his weapon in both hands, pointing it at the hatches as he approached them.

Now Arney had reached the far side and had exited the tunnel. Over the short-com, he said, "Something's going on here. Checking it out."

There was a moment's silence and then Arney was on the radio again. "Got the main floor cleared."

Jefferson waved a hand and the second squad began to trot down the tunnel. They reached a short ridge in the floor that reached from one wall to the other. They stepped over it and kept moving toward the mouth of the tunnel. They slowed as they reached the exit, wanting to make sure it was safe to come out. Arney hadn't warned of an ambush, but Jefferson had learned never to take anything for granted.

As they approached, Jefferson realized they were entering another section of the building that was the mirror image of the one they had passed through. He stopped short and took a moment to study what was ahead of him. And then without seeing any movement except that of the first squad, Jefferson exited into the open.

At the far end, it looked as if the building had been opened. Cold air was blowing in and snow was swirling around the railings of the balconies, the sculpture, and down into the lower levels. It was drifting along the floor and piling up against the walls. It was nearly as cold inside that section of the building as it had been on the outside.

There were lights dancing at the far end and Jefferson realized they were looking at lasers being fired out into the open area. They had found the enemy.

Finally.

21

WITH PEEL MISSING and presumed dead, Lieutenant Colonel Roger Machlin took over command of the regiment. He was trapped on one of the side-streets that lead to the citadel with most of one company. Each time someone tried to move, a dozen weapons opened fire, the beams flashing and the snow sizzling as it melted.

Machlin was a young man, no more than thirty-five. Unlike Peel, he had some combat experience. He'd been under fire, but that had been a primitive planet where they used single-shot, muzzle-loading weapons. Fighting an armed force that had lasers was a different proposition.

He watched as two soldiers tried to melt a hole in the wall with their lasers so they could get into the room next door. The wall absorbed the beams, heating slowly.

He turned and moved to the doorway and then looked out. There were bodies sprawled in the street, the snow beginning to cover them. The lasers from the citadel pinned them down. The beams flashed up the street as if they were searching for the soldiers.

"Sir," said a trooper, "I think Homland is dead."

Machlin moved away from the door and crouched over the

body of the wounded man. The mesh had been overloaded and had burned the man. As it melted, the beams punched through it, burning through Homland's chest and lungs.

"Cover his face," said Machlin.

"Yes, sir."

Over the short-com, he heard, "They're coming at us again."

"Say location," said Machlin.

"Company D, Third Battalion."

Machlin used his heads-up and tried to spot that company. They were over two streets. Machlin poked his head out the door and tried to spot the assault, but the angles were wrong. He couldn't see a thing.

A laser fired at him. The beams slashed through the snow, struck the ground and reflected up in a cloud of steam as it had hit.

"*Here they come!*" yelled one of the men.

Machlin wheeled around and opened fire. He ducked back, shot again and ducked. The enemy fired at him. The beams struck the wall near him.

Others started to shoot. More beams filled the air. A dozen, two dozen, and then a hundred of the enemy entered the street. They attacked the buildings one at a time, forcing their way in. Bodies of the enemy piled up around the doors as they fought to get in. Then, moments after entering, the enemy ran back out to attack another doorway.

"*Coming at us!*" yelled one man.

"Keep firing," said Machlin. Then, "Grenades! Hit them with grenades!"

He dropped his rifle and yanked a grenade free of its pouch. He pulled the pin and dropped it to the floor. Yelling, "Fire in the hole!" he threw the grenade.

It detonated in the middle of the onrushing enemy soldiers. The snow and dirt fountained up. There were screams and then another two explosions. But the enemy fired at the doorways. Machlin had to duck. He grabbed his rifle and without aiming, began shooting out into the street.

The man next to him was hit by a laser. The man fell and rolled clear, but the laser seemed to follow him. Machlin spotted the enemy soldier and shot at him. He hit the enemy in the head and the beam went out.

As the man scrambled to his feet, he yelled, "Thanks." But before he could reclaim his position, he was hit again. His powerpack began to scream. The man turned and the beam cut across his exposed fingers, slicing them from his hand.

For a moment, the man stared at the smoking stubbs that had been his fingers. Then he screamed, dropping his rifle to the floor. A second beam hit him in the back but he didn't move. The mesh melted and failed and the beam punched into his lungs and baked his heart. He fell forward, dead.

Machlin ignored the dead man. He watched as the enemy swarmed toward him. They were clearing the buildings one by one. Machlin turned and said, "They're coming at us."

As the men and women with him tried to stop the assault, Machlin was on the short-com. "Pawnee Three, this is Five."

"Go Five."

"We're about to be overrun. Command is falling to you. Prepare to withdraw the regiment."

"Yes, sir. Understand we are to retreat."

"Roger!" yelled Machlin. "*Get the hell out!*"

There was another question, but Machlin didn't hear it. He was busy then. The enemy was coming straight at him, screaming their rage at him. He fired, the beams of his laser stabbing into the gentle snowfall. He knocked down two of the enemy. His soldiers around him also fired, killing many of the creatures.

But there were too many of them coming too fast. They reached the doorway, forcing Machlin and his tiny band of defenders to retreat. Machlin was caught in the open, between the front door and the exit. He went to one knee, firing all the while. One of the enemy fell in the doorway, but those behind leaped over the body. One of them collided with Machlin, knocking him to his back. Before he could fight back, a dozen laser beams hit him, superheating his uniform. Machlin was baked in a matter of seconds, dying as his body ruptured in the fierce heat.

Franz ran forward, found a shallow depression and dived into it, nearly covering herself with the snow. She slid forward, looking over the rim of the depression.

Cooper, holding his injured arm so he didn't jar his shoulder, stayed crouched at the side of a building. He watched as Franz turned and waved at him. He didn't want to move. He was tired and sore and sick. The pain was making him sweat and once or twice, when his foot hit wrong or he bumped into the side of a building, he'd thought he was going to pass out.

Franz rolled to her side, looked at Cooper, and waved at him, trying to get him to join her.

For a moment Cooper pretended he couldn't see her. He closed his eyes and wished he was warm, that he was on the ship and that his shoulder didn't hurt.

Over the short-com, he heard, "You can join me now."

Cooper nodded but didn't acknowledge on the radio. He turned and looked at her and forced himself to his feet. Cradling his rifle and his injured arm, he started forward, running for a moment and then slowing to a walk as the pain flared.

He eased himself into the depression and then lay back carefully with his sore shoulder off the ground. He was staring up into the snow.

"Not exactly a military maneuver," said Franz.

"I couldn't do it any better," said Cooper. "I can't run anymore."

Franz looked at him and then reached over, pulling the hood from his face. Cooper's skin was pasty white and sweat dotted his forehead and upper lift.

"You're hurt bad, aren't you?" she said.

"I've been trying to tell you that," he said. "I think something might be broken."

Franz nodded and then turned. She used her image enhancer, studying the landscape in front of her. "I think I can see the rear of the regiment. Probably a rear guard or something. You wait here while I go get help."

"Use the radio," said Cooper. "Call for the help."

Franz shook her head and said, "We're supposed to stay off the radio as much as possible. I'll go get some help. You wait here."

Cooper wasn't in the mood to argue. He nodded and said, "Hurry it up."

Franz pushed herself out of the depression and ran for the closest of the buildings. As she neared it, one soldier stepped out and said, "What're you doing back here?"

"Got separated. I've an injured man with me. Can you give me some help?"

The soldier turned and said, "Couple of you people get out here." To Franz he said, "Lead on."

Franz turned and headed back. As they approached, Cooper struggled to sit up. He grinned at them and said, "Thought you'd never get here."

Franz said, "Broke a couple of bones, I think, when we blew up one of the buildings."

"Don't worry, Sarge," said the man, "we'll get him inside. Got a medic who can take a look at him. If nothing else, be able to warm him up and give him something for the pain."

"That's all I ask," said Cooper.

"Guess the war's over for you," said Franz.

"Looks like it might be over for all of us," said the soldier. "Seems that things are winding down."

Torrence, with two companies from her regiment, fanned out in the citadel and then began scrambling down stairs, searching the lower levels of the building. She could hear the sounds of the boots as the men and women ran down the concrete steps. There were occasional shouts, orders given and received as they searched the structure.

At the bottom of the steps, she halted with half a dozen of her soldiers. Two of them approached the doorway, and while one guarded, the second opened it quickly. As it slammed against the rear wall, the soldiers dived through, but the enemy wasn't there.

"All clear," said one of the soldiers.

Torrence moved forward. It looked like they had found the maintenance basement. It opened into a large area with wide walls and lots of doors.

Torrence stepped through and then turned. "Let's get this area cleared," she shouted.

Immediately there was a voice from one of the rooms. "Hey! Hey!"

It was a rusty-sounding voice, like one that was no longer used to speaking English. "Hey! Who is there?"

Torrence had dived to the floor and crawled to the right so she was up against a wall. Her weapon was pointed at the sound. The rest of the soldiers had also jumped for cover.

Torrence glanced at the point man and waited. He got to his feet and then, with his back to the wall, began to work his way down the corridor.

Finally, after he'd gone twenty or thirty feet, he called out, "Is anyone there?"

"Right here. Get me out."

The point man ran forward and grabbed the handle on the door. He lifted it, turned it and then threw the door open. It slammed back against the wall with a dull thud.

The cell was a six-by-six room with a cot attached to the far wall. There was a hole in the floor to be used as a latrine. There was no sink or source of water.

The man in the cell looked to be young and fairly healthy. He stood up, his long hair partially hiding his face. He stood flatfooted with wide open eyes. "Who in the hell are you?"

"Sergeant Patrick Webster, United States Army."

"Good God!" said the man. "I never thought you'd be able to find me."

Webster turned and yelled, "I've got one here."

Suddenly there were more shouts in the corridor. A dozen voices demanded to know what had happened. What was going on there.

Torrence was on her feet. She backed toward the stairway and used the short-com. "We've located some of the prisoners. I want Delta down here now."

"Yes, ma'am. On the way."

She moved back into the corridor and watched as her soldiers ran along the walls, opening door after door. The people were stumbling out of their cells. A few of them looked as if they'd been held for years. Others seemed to have been incarcerated for only weeks or months.

A door at the far end burst open and a dozen of the aliens ran in. They didn't fire but raised sticks above their heads as they screamed at the human prisoners.

"Stop them," yelled Torrence as she went to a knee, firing her laser. The beam slashed through the dim corridor hitting one of the creatures. It tumbled from its feet.

The humans scattered, some running for the safety of their cells. One of them tripped and a guard stood over him, beating him with a wand. Torrence aimed carefully and killed the alien.

In less than thirty seconds, the fight was over, and the creatures were all dead. Two of her soldiers ran forward, checked the bodies quickly and then worked their way toward the door the enemy had used.

"It's clear back here!" yelled one of the soldiers.

"Let's get everyone out of here," said Torrence. "Williams, up the stairs. We've got to clear this area."

The soldiers began clearing the cells, getting the prisoners out of them. They herded people toward the stairs with two of the soldiers bringing up the rear.

Torrence held them there for a moment and then ran up the first flight. She stopped on the landing. Using the short-com, she asked, "Is the main level secure?"

"We've run into no trouble," replied one of the company officers.

Torrence looked back down the stairs. She waved a hand and yelled, "Let's get going!"

She ran up another flight, hesitated, and then walked up the rest of the way. She hesitated again near the top and surveyed the main level. She could see her troops as they had spread throughout the citadel. They were guarding the first floor, including the exit.

She left the stairs and ran along the first level toward the doors. She could see that her regiment held the approaches to the citadel. They held the interior of it and had secured some of the rooms.

"Status here?" she asked one of the officers.

He pointed and said, "We've got people on all levels. Haven't found any evidence that the enemy is here. Appears that the place has been deserted. They've taken almost everything that would be useful to us."

"No sign of the enemy at all?"

"No, ma'am. None."

Torrence nodded and said into the short-com, "Kiowa Six, this is Apache Six."

"Go."

"We've cleared this side of the citadel. We've recovered the prisoners."

"Roger."

"Pulling out now."

"Ah, wait one," said Jefferson on the short-com. Then, "Use two companies to get the people out of here. I want the rest of your regiment to join me on this side of the citadel."

Torrence shrugged and then said, "Roger that. Be there in five minutes."

"Hurry it up," said Jefferson.

"Roger."

22

ONCE JEFFERSON HAD alerted Torrence, he pushed forward with Arney's recon platoon. They ran along the railing, looking down into the pit. They reached the far wall, smashed through a couple of flimsy doors and found themselves in rooms that opened onto the outside. From there, Jefferson could see the battle raging.

"Arney," he said, "Get your people scattered, and once everyone is in position, open fire."

"Yes, sir."

Jefferson walked through one room and crouched near the window. Outside he could see the rear of the enemy formation. They were attacking into the streets. There was return fire from Peel's regiment, but it wasn't as heavy or as well-coordinated as it could have been.

Over the short-com, Jefferson ordered, "On my mark, open fire."

There was no response from the soldiers. None had been required. He gave them enough time to get into position and then ordered, "Pick your targets. Aim carefully and make each shot count. *Take them!*"

He fired then. A single beam flashing out. He didn't see if

it struck anything. He aimed at the rear of the enemy formation, just as the others with him did. Forty separate beams slashing out, cutting into the enemy. A dozen of them fell in the first moments. A few turned and shot back, but their beams hit the walls and were absorbed.

From above, a single beam danced. Jefferson knew what it meant. Someone on the roof. The enemy was up there supporting those in the streets.

Over the short-com, he said, "Apache Six, we've got enemy on the roof."

"Six, roger. We'll take them out."

"Good," said Jefferson. "And get me some additional support here."

"On the way."

Jefferson continued to fire into the rear of the enemy formation. They seemed to ignore him and his soldiers, pressing on into the streets, using the cover there. A few shot back, but in seconds they were gone.

"After them," yelled someone over the short-com.

"Negative," said Jefferson. "Wait for the reinforcements from Apache Six."

"Roger."

Jefferson switched to the long-com. "Pawnee Six, this is Kiowa Six." He waited and when there was no response, said, "Pawnee Five, this is Six." Again there was no response. "Pawnee Three."

"This is Pawnee Three."

"Roger. Kiowa Six. Say status."

"We have taken heavy casualties. Five is dead and Six is missing."

"Say location."

"We have tried to form a line of defense along the original line of departure. Enemy resistance has been heavy but is falling off."

"Are you in danger of being overrun?" asked Jefferson.

"Negative. We have stabilized the line though there is still heavy pressure in the center."

Jefferson keyed his heads-up, got the map and determined where the enemy was attacking.

"We will move to support you in one-five minutes. Can you hold?"

"Roger. We're in good shape now."

Jefferson switched back to the short-com. "Apache Six, I'll need one battalion."

"Roger. I've one coming through the tunnel to your location now."

"Thank you." Jefferson switched back to the long-com. "Sioux Six, this is Kiowa Six."

"Go."

"You'll need to turn your regiment ninety degrees to the right."

"Can do, Six."

"You'll hit the flank and roll up it as far as you can. Be advised that Pawnee regiment is being heavily pressed and is in the area."

"We are ready to relieve them," said Sioux Six.

"Roger. Wait for my command to attack."

"Yes, sir."

Jefferson used his image enhancer to study the scene in front of him. The enemy had disappeared, taking cover in the buildings there. He wished he could call in artillery or air strikes, but he wasn't sure exactly where his people were hiding. They'd have to clear it themselves.

An officer entered the room, ducked out of the line of fire and worked his way toward Jefferson while trying not to expose himself to the enemy outside. As he got close, he said, "Major Malone, General."

"Major."

"We're ready when you are."

Jefferson nodded and took another look outside. It was beginning to brighten. The snow was ending. If they waited, they'd have to attack across an open field without the cover of darkness.

On the short-com, Jefferson said, "Let's go."

Jefferson stood and put one foot up on the sill and jumped through. He landed and went to one knee. He got to his feet and began to run across the field, leaping the bodies of those killed earlier.

He reached the fence line and dropped immediately to the ground. He fired once. The beam hit one of the buildings, but the enemy shot back. A half-dozen of them. Jefferson ducked and felt like laughing. If they'd held their fire, he wouldn't have known where they were.

On the short-com, he said, "Sioux Six, are you in position yet?"

"Roger. Ready to go."

"Move now," said Jefferson.

"Roger."

Nesmith and three companies from her first battalion were spread out along the cross-streets and the buildings that bordered the area occupied by Peel's regiment. They had crept into position, moving carefully through the snow, ignoring the cold and the wind. Over the short-com, they reported one by one that they were ready for the attack.

Nesmith used the long-com. "You are cleared to move. Be sure of your targets."

With that, Nesmith left the shelter of the doorway where she had been hiding. She slid along the wall of the building until she came to the cross-street. She turned down it and fell in behind a platoon of soldiers working its way toward the enemy.

They ran forward with soldiers sprinting ahead to cover the cross-streets. Nesmith glanced down one of the streets as she ran by, but there was no movement along it.

Then ahead, two of the soldiers dived for cover. One of them rolled up on his right side and waved at those behind him, stopping them.

On the short-com, Nesmith asked, "What have we got?"

"Enemy in the street."

"Can you take them out?"

"Not easily. We'll need some help."

Nesmith was going to order a squad forward, but before she could speak, the men and women began to move. Now it was slower, with each soldier covering his partner. They leapfrogged down the street, taking firing positions.

"You may fire when ready." Nesmith began to ease her way forward toward the skirmish line. As she approached, she got to her belly and crawled forward. She noticed that the snow was as cold as that on Earth.

She reached the corner and stuck her head around it. She could see the beams of the lasers flashing, though they were dimmer than they had been with the coming of the sun. The enemy, caught in the open, was trying to withdraw, but there weren't enough of them for a rear-guard action. Before Nesmith could fire her weapon, the last of the enemy soldiers died.

One of the soldiers was up and running then. He crossed the street and threw himself to the ground. He rolled once and came up ready to fire again, but there was no one shooting at him.

Over the short-com, the soldier reported, "Street now clear."

Nesmith said, "Let's go, people."

Jefferson didn't wait. He was up and moving immediately, firing from the hip as the rest of the company moved with him. They hit the street and spread out, firing into the enemy formations. For a moment the enemy didn't know they were there. They continued to assault the remnants of Peel's regiment. And then suddenly they saw the new attack. Without a command, they turned, running down the street.

Jefferson and his soldiers followed, keeping up the pressure. Jefferson ran down the center of the street, chasing the enemy. He stopped once, fired, and then began running again. He tried to ignore the damage done to the buildings on either side because he knew it would mean the deaths of his soldiers.

They kept moving, chasing the enemy. Jefferson could hear the shouts of people around him. They were calling out orders or calling for help. Some of them were just screaming their rage.

Jefferson reached the cross-street and slipped to a halt. He raised his rifle to fire, but the targets had all disappeared. Around him were the bodies of the dead enemy and his soldiers and those of Nesmith's regiment. It had been a brief, deadly firefight.

One of the soldiers approached Jefferson. "That's it, General. We got them all." He was breathing hard. He reached up and pulled his hood from his head and wiped the sweat from his face. It looked strange to see a soldier sweating heavily in a snowstorm.

Jefferson looked at the bodies, wisps of smoke blowing in the light breeze. The sun was up and the snow had slowed to flurries. It was easy to see the city now and the damage done to it.

Over the long-com, Jefferson said, "I need a situation report here."

"This is Apache Six. We've cleared the citadel. We've got the prisoners out."

"Roger. Pawnee Three?"

"We've broken contact. I'm attempting to withdraw now."

"All units return to rally points for pickup," said Jefferson.

"Apache Six, roger."

"Sioux Six, roger."

"Pawnee Three, roger."

Jefferson moved back toward one of the buildings. He watched as the soldiers began to filter out of the city. One platoon held back as a rear guard, watching for the enemy. There was no longer any reason to hold where they were. It was time to clear out and let the fleet take care of the enemy's defensive positions that hadn't been destroyed.

Jefferson waited for a moment and then said to Arney, "Let's get our people out of here."

"Yes, sir."

Jefferson fell in with the men and women. They stayed close to the buildings, but they were moving faster now. Without the snowfall to worry about, with the enemy cleared from the city, and now that the sun was up, it was easier to move. And since they were heading to the pickup zones, they were more enthusiastic about it.

They were trotting, one soldier guarding the cross-streets as the rest of the platoon crossed. That soldier would then fall in with the platoon, working with the rear guard.

In thirty minutes they were clear of the city. They poured out onto an open plain. They fanned out into a loose circle so they could protect one another.

Jefferson used the long-com, "Hornet Six, this is Kiowa Six."

"Go."

"We're ready for the pickup. One platoon."

"Roger. About thirty minutes. Say status of the pickup zone."

"It's cold."

"Roger that."

Arney approached. "We're set. Perimeter is established."

Jefferson nodded. "Now all we've got to do is keep warm until the shuttle gets here."

"Shouldn't be a problem," said Arney. He hesitated and then added quickly, "I didn't think it would be that easy."

"Wasn't all that easy," said Jefferson.

"Yes, sir. Is there anything else?"

"No."

Arney left Jefferson standing alone in the center of the tiny perimeter. All he could think of were Arney's words and then the deaths of the men and women who had brought about the successful completion of the mission. Their bodies were scattered around the industrial complex the enemy had surrendered to them.

"No," he repeated. "Wasn't all that easy."

23

JEFFERSON WAS ONE of the first off the shuttle once it was docked with the ship. He stood for a moment, looking at the assembled sailors and crew and at Garvey, who stood near the hatch with his video gear running.

As soon as Jefferson was clear of the shuttle, Garvey shouted, "What the hell happened?"

Jefferson turned back, looking at the shuttle, and watched as Torrence exited. Her uniform was torn at the shoulder and she'd pulled her hood off. Her hair, chopped short to accommodate the hood, was sticking up in a couple of places.

She glanced at Garvey and then back to Jefferson. "That's a very good question. What in the hell did happen?"

Jefferson spotted the officer of the deck. He waved at the woman and said, "Get some of the medical people down here. We've got wounded and some of the prisoners. All need medical attention."

"Aye aye, General."

One of the wounded men looked up and said, "How'd it go, General?"

Jefferson stopped. "Went just fine. Kicked their butts. . . ."

"Corporal Cooper, sir." He waved his good hand. "Did this to myself, diving out a door."

"Guess we'll have to teach you to be more careful."

"Yes, sir."

Jefferson turned then and to Torrence said, "Let's go find Carter and see if he's got any answers."

Garvey's camera was still running as the noise level on the shuttle deck continued to build. More soldiers dropped from the shuttle and more sailors ran to get equipment secured and prepare the shuttle bay for the arrival of the next ship.

Jefferson, with Torrence it tow, headed for a hatch. It irised open and they stepped through. Garvey had turned to tape their departure. As the hatch closed and the noise level suddenly dropped, Torrence said, "Glad we're out of that."

A sailor appeared and said, "The captain invites you to the bridge, General."

"Thank you," Jefferson said. "Please tell the captain that I, and Colonel Torrence, will be there in a moment. We've a couple of things to do."

"Aye, sir. I'll tell the captain."

Together Jefferson and Torrence walked to the mid-lift. They took it toward the brigade's office deck and got off. They walked to the intelligence office and found Carter sitting there, studying the flatscreens.

"Major," said Jefferson.

Carter leaped to his feet and grinned. "Welcome back, General."

"I've just one question for you," said Jefferson. "What in the hell happened?"

Carter shot a glance over his shoulder at the large center flatscreen. Then, to Jefferson, he said, "I think you ran into the rear guard."

"What?"

The second man in the room, wearing a flightsuit that looked to have just been pulled from supply, new sandals, and a baseball cap, said, "A rear guard. They got out as quickly as they could."

Jefferson turned his attention to the new man. "You're Carson, right?"

"Yes, General. Shot down on the planet, sure that I was falling into a hotbed of enemy soldiers, but hell, no one bothered me. SAR slipped in, picked me up and brought me back here."

"Glad you got out," said Jefferson.

"Thank you, General."

"Carter, what in the hell is going on?"

Carter turned and walked toward the screen. He leaned to the right and pushed a series of buttons and then pointed up at the screen. "We've watched the enemy launch ships, make no real attempt to attack us, and flee from the system."

"And there was no real resistance on the ground," said Torrence.

"Except for that bunch that Peel hit."

Torrence spoke for the first time. "Peel. That asshole."

"He got his," said Jefferson. Peel's body had been found near the citadel. Given the situation, that Peel had disobeyed orders, it worked out for the best. Now Jefferson didn't have to deal with Peel. The enemy had done it for him.

Carter said, "What it looks like is that they've been evacuating the system since you turned their expeditionary force around in that last battle a couple of months ago. We ran into the last of them. If we'd stayed away another month or two, we might not have run into any of them."

Jefferson suddenly felt dizzy. Once again the vision of the dead swam in front of him. Soldiers killed because they had thought they needed to attack.

"The prisoners," said Torrence.

"Well, we don't know what they would have done. I suspect they'd have left them behind to fend for themselves. Or they might have just killed them."

"Wait a minute," said Jefferson. "I thought this was their home world."

Carter shrugged. "That was the information we had, but it looks like it was wrong."

"Shit!" said Jefferson. "I thought this thing was going to be over."

Carter took a deep breath. "They're getting out. They ran before we could get here. I don't think we need to worry about them anymore. I think this thing is over. As of now."

"I'll check with division," said Jefferson.

"Certainly, General," said Carter, "but my information comes from the division intel officer. He's been with the CO. It's based on observations from them."

Jefferson turned and pulled at one of the chairs. He dropped into it. "I don't believe it."

"You can," said Carter. "It's based on the observations of every ship in the fleet and on the intelligence gathered by the scouts. It's solid information."

"I can't believe they'd abandon the system."

"The evidence is in front of you, General," said Carter. "I can play the tapes showing their ships getting out. Very little engagement with our ships. They were running and the fighting that did take place was to protect the majority of the ships as they evacuated." He pointed at Carson and added, "Even Carson had no trouble getting out. No one cared about him."

Carson raised his Coke can. "Except the boys and girls with the SAR forces."

"Good people," said Torrence.

"There are no indications of enemy presence anywhere in this system," Carter said. "We've been probing with everything at our command. Scouts have landed on each of the planets and most of the moons. The enemy has gone."

Jefferson let the information sink in. He stared up at the screens that were replaying at a fast speed the tapes that had been made showing the enemy evacuation. There was nothing to indicate the enemy had remained. Or that the enemy was going to fight. The battle, and maybe the war, was over. The information began to sink in slowly.

As the silence lengthened, Torrence moved closer to Jefferson. "General," she said.

"That's it, Vicki," he said quickly. "We might be out of a job."

"I don't think so," she said.

Jefferson suddenly grinned. "I do. I think this calls for a celebration. A real celebration."

"Yes, sir." Torrence was still trying to accept the fact. She wasn't sure how to react. Carter seemed to be very calm. Jefferson seemed to be more than calm. He looked to be years younger and was suddenly relaxed, as if a weight had been lifted from his shoulders.

"And I think we'd better tell the troops. They've got the right to know." He laughed and said, "Damn. I think I do believe this now. I think we made it."

"Yes, David," said Torrence, now convinced as she watched the tapes. "That we did."

"_The Night Whistlers_ will keep you hypnotized. It's frightening fiction that poses realistic questions."
—Bob Ham, author of _Overload_

The second American Revolution is about to begin...

THE NIGHT WHISTLERS
Dan Trevor

Freedom is dead in the year 2030. Megacorporations rule with a silicon fist, and citizen-slaves toil ceaselessly under the sadistic watch of Corporate Security. In a world enslaved, they're fighting back. The dream of liberty lives on for John Gray and his revolutionary platoon. In the darkness of the night, the Whistlers are taking back the battle-scarred streets—and giving America back to the people.

_THE NIGHT WHISTLERS 0-515-10663-1/$3.99

For Visa, MasterCard and American Express orders ($10 minimum) call: 1-800-631-8571

FOR MAIL ORDERS: CHECK BOOK(S). FILL OUT COUPON. SEND TO:	POSTAGE AND HANDLING: $1.50 for one book, 50¢ for each additional. Do not exceed $4.50.
BERKLEY PUBLISHING GROUP 390 Murray Hill Pkwy., Dept. B East Rutherford, NJ 07073	**BOOK TOTAL** $ ____
NAME_____	**POSTAGE & HANDLING** $ ____
ADDRESS_____	**APPLICABLE SALES TAX** $ ____ (CA, NJ, NY, PA)
CITY_____	**TOTAL AMOUNT DUE** $ ____
STATE_____ ZIP_____	**PAYABLE IN US FUNDS.** (No cash orders accepted.)
PLEASE ALLOW 6 WEEKS FOR DELIVERY. PRICES ARE SUBJECT TO CHANGE	365

From the writer of Marvel Comics' bestselling *X-Men* series.

CHRIS CLAREMONT

The explosive sequel to *FirstFlight*

GROUNDED!

Lt. Nicole Shea was a top space pilot—until a Wolfpack attack left her badly battered. Air Force brass say she's not ready to return to space, so they reassign her to a "safe" post on Earth. But when someone begins making attempts on her life, she must travel back into the stars, where memories and threats linger. It's the only way Shea can conquer her fears—and win back her wings.

___0-441-30416-8/$4.95

For Visa, MasterCard and American Express orders ($10 minimum) call: 1-800-631-8571

FOR MAIL ORDERS: CHECK BOOK(S). FILL OUT COUPON. SEND TO:	POSTAGE AND HANDLING: $1.50 for one book, 50¢ for each additional. Do not exceed $4.50.
BERKLEY PUBLISHING GROUP 390 Murray Hill Pkwy., Dept. B East Rutherford, NJ 07073	**BOOK TOTAL** $ _____
NAME_____	**POSTAGE & HANDLING** $ _____
ADDRESS_____	**APPLICABLE SALES TAX** $ _____ (CA, NJ, NY, PA)
CITY_____	**TOTAL AMOUNT DUE** $ _____
STATE_____ ZIP_____	**PAYABLE IN US FUNDS.** (No cash orders accepted.)
PLEASE ALLOW 6 WEEKS FOR DELIVERY. PRICES ARE SUBJECT TO CHANGE WITHOUT NOTICE.	383

DAVID DRAKE

__NORTHWORLD__ 0-441-84830

The consensus ruled twelve hundred w... hworld. Three fleets had been dispatched to pr... North-world. None returned. Now, Commiss... must face the challenge of the distant planet. ...ront a world at war, a world of androids...all u...

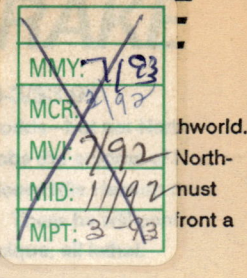

__SURFACE ACTION__ 0-441-36375-X/$4.50

Venus has been transformed into a world of underwater habitats for Earth's survivors. Battles on Venus must be fought on the ocean's exotic surface. Johnnie Gordon trained his entire life for battle, and now his time has come to live a warrior's life on the high seas.

THE FLEET Edited by David Drake and Bill Fawcett

The soldiers of the Human/Alien Alliance come from different worlds and different cultures. But they share a common mission: to reclaim occupied space from the savage Khalian invaders.

__BREAKTHROUGH__   0-441-24105-0/$3.95
__COUNTERATTACK__   0-441-24104-2/$3.95
__SWORN ALLIES__   0-441-24090-9/$3.95

For Visa, MasterCard and American Express orders ($10 minimum) call: 1-800-631-8571

FOR MAIL ORDERS: CHECK BOOK(S). FILL OUT COUPON. SEND TO:

BERKLEY PUBLISHING GROUP
390 Murray Hill Pkwy., Dept. B
East Rutherford, NJ 07073

NAME_____
ADDRESS_____
CITY_____
STATE_____ ZIP_____

PLEASE ALLOW 6 WEEKS FOR DELIVERY.
PRICES ARE SUBJECT TO CHANGE WITHOUT NOTICE.

POSTAGE AND HANDLING:
$1.50 for one book, 50¢ for each additional. Do not exceed $4.50.

BOOK TOTAL $ _____
POSTAGE & HANDLING $ _____
APPLICABLE SALES TAX $ _____
(CA, NJ, NY, PA)
TOTAL AMOUNT DUE $ _____
PAYABLE IN US FUNDS.
(No cash orders accepted.)

317